SHOWING
THE
FLAG

SHOWING
THE
FLAG

AND OTHER STORIES

BY

JANE GARDAM

Hamish Hamilton
London

HAMISH HAMILTON LTD

Published by the Penguin Group
27 Wrights Lane, London W8 5TZ, England
Viking Penguin Inc, 40 West 23rd Street, New York, New York 10010, U.S.A.
Penguin Books Australia Ltd, Ringwood, Victoria, Australia
Penguin Books Canada Ltd, 2801 John Street, Markham, Ontario, Canada L3R 1B4
Penguin Books (N.Z.) Ltd, 182–190 Wairau Road, Auckland 10, New Zealand

Penguin Books Ltd, Registered Offices: Harmondsworth, Middlesex, England

First published in Great Britain 1989 by
Hamish Hamilton Ltd

SHOWING THE FLAG First published in *Winter's Tales*, Constable 1987
BENEVOLENCE First published in *Winter's Tales*, Constable 1986
BANG, BANG – WHO'S DEAD First published in *Beware, Beware*, Hamish Hamilton 1987
THREADS First published in *Misfits* edited by Peggy Woodford, The Bodley Head 1984
RODE BY ALL WITH PRIDE First published in *London Tales*, Hamish Hamilton 1983
SWAN First published by Julia MacRae 1987

1 3 5 7 9 10 8 6 4 2

British Library Cataloguing in Publication Data

Gardam, Jane, *1928–*
Showing the flag.
1. Great Britain.   Social aspects.
I. Title
823'914 [F]

ISBN 0–241–12727–0

Printed and bound in Great Britain by
Butler & Tanner Ltd, Frome and London

For Bruce Hunter

CONTENTS

SHOWING THE FLAG

THE boy with big ears, whose father was dead, kissed his mother with a sliding away of the eyes, heaved up his two immense suit-cases and loped up the gang-plank. At the top he dropped the cases briefly to give a quick sideways wave, keeping his face forward. He jerked the cases up again, grimaced, tramped on and his mother far below, weeping but laughing, said, "Oh, Pym! It's the size of the cases. They're nearly as big as he is. Oh, I can't bear it."

"He is going for a sensible time," said her elderly woman friend. "Three months is a good long time. The cases must necessarily be heavy."

"I can't bear it," wept the other, dabbing her streaming cheeks, laughing at her weakness.

"Of course you can. You must. It's not as if he's never been away before."

"Since six. He's been away since he was six. Oh, boarding-schools. Oh, children – why does one have them? Children – it's all renunciation. Having them is just learning to give them up."

"It is the custom of the country," said the elderly friend – unmarried. She was a Miss Pym. "It is in the culture of the English middle class. We teach our children how to endure."

"He has endured. He has learned."

"Oh, he scarcely knew his father, Gwen. Don't be silly. His father was hardly ever at home."

"He missed him. Not of course as I – "

"You scarcely saw him either," said sane Miss Pym. She was a plain-spoken woman.

"I loved him," said Gwen, impressive in her heavy hanging musquash coat and flat velvet bandeau (it was the nineteen-

1

twenties). "And now I have lost Philip. Oh, can we find tea?"
She held her tightly-squeezed handkerchief in her fist, out in
front of her like a blind woman, and her friend led her away
through the crowds, among the crates and high-piled luggage
and the other fluttering handkerchiefs. Arm in arm the two
women disappeared, slowly, floppily in their expensive boat-
shaped shoes, and Philip who had found a good position for
the suit-cases beside a long slatted seat, hung over the rail and
waved to them in vain.

When the last flicker of them had gone he blew through his
teeth a bit until a whistle came and swung his feet at the
bottom rail along the deck, scuffing his shoes like a two-year-
old, though he was nearly thirteen. As the ship got away
towards France he hung further over the rail and called down
at the sea-gulls who were wheeling and screeching round the
open port-hole of the galley. A bucket of scraps was flung out.
The sea-gulls screamed at it and caught most of it before it hit
the foam. They plunged. "Hungry," thought Philip. "I'm
hungry. I hope the food's going to be good. Messy French
stuff. They all say it's going to be good, but it'll be no better
than school. It's just disguised school."

"The sea-gulls eat like school." He watched enviously the
birds tearing horrors from each other's beaks, flying free.
Were they French or English sea-gulls? Where did they nest?
They spoke a universal language, sea-gulls. And all birds.
All animals. Presumably. Didn't need to learn French.
"They're ahead of people," thought Philip covering his great
red ears.

It was bitterly cold. Maybe it would be warmer in Paris.

He was to get to Paris on the boat-train by himself and
would there be met by a Major Foster. They would know one
another by a small paper union-jack pinned to a lapel on each
of them. Philip was keeping his union-jack in his coat pocket
at present, in a small brass tin. Every few minutes he felt the
tin to make sure that it was still there.

He left the rail and sat on the long seat beside the suit-cases.

2

He could not remember actually having seen the flag in the tin, only hearing about it there. He had seen it when it was part of a small packet of union-jacks, tied in a bundle. He had heard nothing else but union-jacks it seemed for weeks: his mother's search for just the right one, the dispatch of the Major's identical one to Paris with the instructions to him about the lapel. The (rather long) wait for the letter of confirmation from the Major that the union-jack had been safely received. Then a further letter about the *positioning* of the union-jack on the *right* lapel, in the centre and with a gold safety-pin.

Philip however could not remember the act of placing the union-jack inside the tin. After all, she might just have forgotten. Not that it was the sort of thing she ever did do – forget. But during the last few months – after the funeral which he hadn't gone to, and which she hadn't gone to, being too ill in bed and her friend Miss Pym paddling about nursing her and bossing her in a darkened room – after the funeral there had been some sort of break. Only a short break of course. His mother wasn't one to break. She was terrific, his mother. Everyone knew she was terrific. She kept everything right. Never made a mistake. Ace organiser. He'd heard them saying in the kitchen that it was her being so perfect had killed his father, though goodness knows, thought Philip, what that meant.

Oh, his mother was a whizz. Organising, packing, making decisions. "These are your gifts. These are your life-blood," had said Miss Pym. "You are by nature an administrator – quite wasted now as a mere mother." His school matron always sighed over his trunk at the end of term. "However did your mother get so much *in*?" she said. There was not a shoe not filled with socks, not a sock that did not hide a card of special darning-wool or extra buttons. Bundles of Cash's name-tapes would be folded into a face flannel. Soap in a little soap-shaped celluloid box would rest inside a cocoa mug, and the cocoa mug would rest inside a cricket cap and the cricket

3

cap would be slid into a wellington boot.

No. She'd never have forgotten the union-jack.

"I think it's rather a lot to expect of a Frenchman," had said Miss Pym. "To wear the English flag."

"The Fosters are French-Canadian," had said his mother. "They're very English. Very patriotic, although they live in the Avenue Longchamps."

"I hope their French is not patriotic. If so there's very little point in Philip going."

"They are patriotic to France as well."

"How odd," said Pym. "That is unusual."

Philip took the tin out of his pocket and shook it and there seemed to be no rattle from inside. But then when he opened the lid, there lay the little paper flag quite safe beside its pin and the wind at once scooped it up and blew it away among the sea-gulls.

Philip ran to the rail and watched it plucked outwards and upwards, up and up, then round and down. Down it went, a little bright speck until it became invisible in the churning sea.

"*Calais*," said the fat French lady along the seat beside him. "You see? Here is France." Philip immediately got up and walked away. He looked at the scummy waves slopping at the green jetty, the tall leaning houses. There was a different smell. This was abroad. Foreign soil. In a moment he was going to set foot upon it.

And he was lost and would never be found.

"*Le petit*," said the French lady coming up alongside him at the rail and stroking his hair. He wagged his head furiously and moved further away. "*Tout seul*," and she burst into a spate of French at her husband. Philip knew that the French meant that the barbaric English had abandoned this child. Not able to consider this concept he shouldered the suit-cases and made for the quay, and there was approached by a ruffian who tried to take them both from him. He hung on to them

4

tight, even when the man began to scream and shout. He aimed a kick at the man and tramped away, the cases grazing the ground. Not one person on the crowded quay paid attention to the attempted theft.

Philip showed his passport and was swirled into the crowd. "*Paris*," cried the fat lady, swinging into view, "*Paris – ah, le petit!*" and she held her rounded arm out boldly but shelteringly in his direction, leaning towards him. Her husband who had a sharp nose and black beret and teeth began to talk fast and furiously into the nearest of Philip's vulnerable ears.

But Philip behaved as though he were quite alone. He climbed into the train, found his seat, took off his gaberdine rain-coat, folded it onto a little rack and looked at the huge suit-cases and the higher luggage-rack with nonchalance. The rest of the carriage regarded them with amazement and several people passionately urged that the racks were unequal to the challenge ahead of them. Another ruffian came in and seemed to want to remove the cases altogether but Philip with a vehemence that astonished him and the ruffian and the whole carriage and a stretch of the corridor, flung himself in the man's path and across his property. He turned bright red and his ears redder and cried out, "No, no, no".

This caused more discussion and the ruffian, lifting his gaze to the ceiling and his hands near it, went shouting away. The suit-cases were then successfully stowed on the racks, two of the Frenchmen shook hands with Philip and an old woman wearing a long black dress and a lace head-dress like some sort of queen, offered him a sweet which he refused. Huddled in his corner seat he looked out of the window and wondered what to do.

Rattling tracks, bleak cement, scruffy houses all tipping about and needing a coat of paint. Shutters. Railway lines insolently slung across streets, all in among fruit-stalls, all muddly. Rain. No union-jack.

Rain. Fields. Grey. Everything measured out by rulers.

5

Small towns, now villages. Gardens. Allotments. No union-jack.

Men in blue overalls. More berets. Black suits. Stout women with fierce brows. Men standing looking at their allotments, very still and concentrated like saying their prayers. Vegetables in very straight rows. Men carefully bending down and plucking out minute, invisible weeds. Mix-up of muddle and order. Like Mother. No union-jack.

What should he do? Major Foster would be wearing his union-jack and Philip would go up to him and say – . But in all the hundreds of people getting off the train at Paris there might be a dozen boys of twelve. Perhaps a hundred. The Major would go sweeping by. "Oh no. I'm sorry. They were very particular. The boy I am to meet will be wearing – ."

And he'd be speaking in French of course. Probably French-Canadians spoke no English. It hadn't been clear. Miss Pym had written all the letters to the Foster family because she could write French, and the replies had been in French. Miss Pym had taken them away to translate with the dictionary under her arm. No union-jack.

How stupid. How *stupid* of his mother. Why hadn't she sewed the union-jack on his raincoat in the first place? She loved sewing. She was always mending and sewing, not even listening to his father and Miss Pym scrapping away about politics, just looking across at them now and then, or looking over, smiling, at him. His socks were more darns than socks because she so loved darning. Loved making things perfect. Loved making everything seem all right.

So then she sends him away with a rotten little Woolworth's union-jack out of a cheap packet of them, loose in a tin. And not waving either when she'd said goodbye. Not crying at all. He knew about that crying-and-laughing-together she did. He'd never thought anything of it. He wondered if it had been the laughing-and-crying and all the darning and soupy Miss Pym and her French that *had* killed his father.

After all, she hadn't really seemed to *mind* his father dying.

6

Gone off to bed for the funeral. Perhaps she'd really wanted him to die. Wanted to be free of him so that she could have long, cosy chats with Miss Pym. Horrible Miss Pym speaking her mind all the time. Not liking his father and showing it. Not liking boys. Not liking him. Goopy-goo about his mother. Organising these Fosters. Very glad he was going away. Making no secret of that.

Perhaps his mother also was glad that he was going away.

Philip when this thought arrived concentrated upon the colourless, hedgeless, straight-edged French fields. Rattle-crash the train went over the level-crossings that sliced the roads in half. Long poles hung with metal aprons. Funny people. Lots of them on bicycles, clustered round, waiting to cross. Very dangerous. Very daring. People full of – what? Different from home. Full of energy. No, not energy – what? Fireworks. Explosives. Confidence. That was it. Not as if they needed to keep private their secret thoughts.

If they suddenly discovered for instance that their mothers did not love them they would not sit dumb and numb in a corner.

People in the carriage were now getting out packets of food. One of the hand-shaking men offered Philip a slanted slice of bread, orange and white. Somebody else offered him wine. He shook his head at all of it and looked out of the window. When the talk in the carriage began to get lively he got up and took down the raincoat and took from the pocket the packet of lunch his mother had made up for him herself, with her own fair hands, ha-ha. He sat with it on his knee. He was too sad, too shy to open it.

Also he didn't really want it. His mother had packed it up so carefully. Like a work of art. Greaseproof corners turned into triangles, like a beautifully-made bed. The package was fastened with two elastic bands, criss-cross, making four neat squares. And even his name on it in clear black pencil. PHILIP. How silly could you get? Who else would it be for? *Madly* careful, that's what she was. And then she goes and leaves the

7

union-jack loose in the box.

And she knew how flimsy it was. She must have expected it to blow away. She expected everything. She'd expected a wind. She'd gone on at breakfast-time about him getting sea-sick. And she knew he'd be more than likely to open the box.

Oh, she'd known what would happen all right. She'd gone off without even waving, her yellow fur arm on the yellow fur arm of Pym. She did not love him, want him, know him and she never had. It was all just darning and being perfect.

She wanted him lost.

All that about flags was just a blind. She *wanted* him to miss the Major. Wanted rid of the bother of him. Wanted him to disappear. She was a wicked woman who had killed her husband. All that laughing as she cried.

One night when he was young Philip had come downstairs after being put to bed, to get a book from the morning-room and through the dining-room door had heard his father singing at table:

Oh me and oh my
  Oh dear and oh dear
  I ain't gonna drink
  No more damned beer

and Miss Pym had come sailing out of the room with her lips pressed together. "Coarse," he had heard her say, "Coarse," and then, seeing him standing in his pyjamas at the foot of the stairs in the summer evening light, "Go to bed, Philip. Don't look so stricken. There is a point when every child sees through his parents."

But his father's singing hadn't make Philip think any less of him. He'd always rather liked his father, or what he saw of him. He'd not been able to talk to children, just looked awkward and done card-tricks. Once in the town seeing his son walking on the other side of the road his father had raised his hat to him. What did she mean "see through"?

But now he was seeing through his mother. He was seeing

8

through her all right. He knew her now. The stupid woman. All that fuss trailing about for flags in Canterbury and then she gets one that blows away. Accidentally-on-purpose-ha-ha. She'd be free now. Free for life. Free to be with Stinkerpym. They'd got rid of him together, making sure the flag was really flimsy. Brilliantly they had evaded the law and there would be no evidence of their plot. Philip the only son would simply disappear.

Well, he wouldn't. At least he would, because he'd never go back. Not to Canterbury, never. Thirteen was all right. He'd manage. Look at *Kidnapped*. Look at *Treasure Island*. You can get on without your mother. When he'd got to Paris he'd –. He had some money. He'd just put up in a hotel for a few nights. Get work. He could probably get work somewhere as a kitchen boy or – well, somewhere where there was food.

He was very hungry now. Probably Major Foster and his sisters would have got a good dinner ready for him. This dinner he would never eat, never see, as he would never see the beautiful house they all said would be like a little palace near the Bois de Boulogne. Too bad. He'd go to the Paris stews. At least they sounded as if you didn't go hungry.

And since he was so hungry at the moment he would eat his mother's sandwiches. She could hardly have poisoned them.

Could she?

As he opened the greaseproof paper he considered the enigma of his mother, how she flitted in and out of his life, always waving him away on trains. Sending him to school at six.

And even now I could fox her, he thought. Even now I could tear a bit off this greaseproof and draw a union-jack on it and pin it on the lapel with the pin in the box. I could write my name on it too. I could borrow a pencil.

He looked round the carriage wondering which of them he might ask. It would be an easy sentence to say. He'd even done it at school. And he had begun to like the look of the

9

French faces.

But no. He'd go to the stews.

He opened the sandwiches and there was an envelope on top and inside it a piece of paper and his mother's huge handwriting saying "Oh Philip, my darling, don't hate me for fussing, but I do so love you."

Pinned to the paper was a spare union-jack.

THE DIXIE GIRLS

EIGHTY years ago, or thereabouts, Nell had shared a governess with the Dixie girls, Vi and V. and May, the daughters of a Major in the Blues and Greys.

It was V. who had been the particular friend. Vi had been five years older and bossy, May, three years younger and rather sharp. Nell, the landlady's daughter, had been in awe of all three of them and fearfully in awe of the parents; Mrs Dixie, a remote, enduring woman sitting upright and frowning at her sewing in an uncomfortable chair, pursing her Scottish lips; and the Major, a voice, a moustache a lubricious gleam, an Olympian shadow springing down the stairs. Major Dixie had been often from home.

The Dixies had been long-term lodgers with Nell's mother in the North Yorkshire town of Pickering, a high cold blowy place near the garrison in the middle of moors. It had suited the Dixies well, for they had come from bracing Peebles. Peebles they had so loved that in Nell's ears it came to be confused sometimes with heaven. She would wonder if she would ever get there.

The governess one day went hastily home to it and after that the governess was Vi, who kept a page or so ahead of V. and May and Nell, reading everything up an hour before the lesson. Nell's mother was not charged for her daughter's education but the rent of the Dixies was reduced from twenty-five shillings a week to sixteen (family rate, food, heating inclusive) though this was never mentioned. The Dixies somehow made it clear to Nell that they were being good to her.

They saw to her Yorkshire accent for a start. Nell at over eighty, lying in the dark sometimes, and thinking of her days in the school-room – that is to say in her mother's dining-room; cruets on the sideboard, woolly mats, a malicious, razor-toothed plant, dry as buckram on a tall jardinière in the window – Nell saw more clearly than her recent landscapes the Dixie girls all twisting and squirming with glee at her voice. "Bread and serrip. Bread and serrip." She remembered her blush and sometimes so intensely that she blushed again. Blushing is rare in the old. She saw again behind the rosy bobble curtains and the governess's wretched face the white light of the moors. She heard the north wind over the scratchy black heather.

The Dixies all went away, following the flag, following the Major. Nell lived on for years in Pickering and kept on with helping at home where officers' families were always coming and going. During the Great War she married a batman of one of these officers and afterwards settled with him in Leeds. He was a cobbler, a silent man who had survived the Somme. They had a baby daughter.

Nell however did not lose touch with the formidable Dixie family since the one thing that the white-faced governess had instilled in her – apart from the unacceptability of the Yorkshire accent – was the necessity of Correspondence to a civilised life. The first duty of the day for a woman – unless of course she were of the servant class – was to attend to her letters.

This as it happened was entirely to Nell's taste and she would probably have done it anyway, for she was a creature so formed that she felt nothing to have properly occurred unless she had communicated it in writing. Writing to people about other people was her relish and her huge delight and though she could not manage to write as she had been taught, straight after breakfast and for the first post, after the slop-pails, the scrubbing brush, the possing-tub, the mangle, the range, the scouring of pans with soda, the black-leading of the grate, the brasses, the making of dinner for herself and the cobbler and Hilda the robust baby and the clearing of

12

everything up, down she would sit to her letters. She wrote with a smile upon her face or with lips tight with emotion, with frown-lines of righteous indignation and sometimes even with tears a-flow. The most minute events of the terrace in Leeds were made radiant by Nell and born earlier or later she might well have been advised to branch out and become a novelist, brimming as she did with such immediacy.

As it was, she had a very happy time and the Dixie girls as the unselfconscious pages flowed forth from Leeds into India, Kenya, Malta, Basingstoke, Cyprus, Aden, Cheltenham and Singapore called out to each other, "Here's dear Nell again," raising amused eye-brows. They always read the letters, often two or three times, and V. who was the chief recipient kept many of them in a box. "Dear Nell," they all said to each other, "*Such* excitements." There was a slight uneasiness in their voices sometimes – or at least in the voice of Vi or May – that Nell should be so entertaining, so articulate, so full of gusto. Was it not just a bit *forward* of her to write with such self-confidence? But V., who was nice, said not at all. She looked forward to dear Nell's pretty handwriting on an envelope. "Well, she owes that to *us*," said Vi.

V. – it was short for Victoria – replied to Nell's letters very dutifully, as she too had been taught; never starting a paragraph with an I, always answering information received point for point before presenting anything new, always remembering to send messages to the cobbler and the baby – never forgetting the baby's birthday. Sometimes she enclosed sprigs of colonial vegetation – a silken purple poppy-flower pressed almost transparent like a butterfly's wing, or a squelched hot orchid from Kuala Lumpur or a dry little shower of bay. The Dixie girls communicated best in symbols, being not much hands at describing. V. alone could now and then wax voluble on the subject that meant most to her, which was her health – or rather her sickness and the sicknesses of others.

Sickness and death. These were the enemy. The Dixie girls

13

who had so upsettingly to their parents not been boys had need of enemies, enemies through whom though they could not be despatched by sword or shot they could demonstrate their bravery.

How very bravely for instance V. set out to do down the onslaughts of the flesh. She ate little, she lived in cold houses, she walked far in bad weather on fragile ankles, she spent almost nothing on clothes; and after her parents' death she returned to England to a freezing address on the Kent coast spending her evenings sewing sides-to-middles of old sheets for charity, and darning for herself, and often writing her delicate letters with fingers blue and pleated at the tip. The Major had died of drink and Mrs Dixie of desiccation. There was no money left. Said V. "We are in penury." Vi had taken a job as a teacher at a dubious private school near Wokingham and May had "taken a job" moving pieces of paper about in an office that had something to do with a kind godfather, and had a bed-sit in Ealing. "We are fallen on hard times," wrote V. to Nell from the pretty Kent cottage beneath her father's fine portrait and before a fire of one small coal. "It is a very good thing that we are Dixies, or we could not bear it."

Nell found this statement totally unsurprising. She had believed for so long that the Dixies were significant that their superiority to everyone she knew was notched in her brain. Dixie to her meant Hohenzollern, Battenberg and Teck. She knew that had the Czar or Charlemagne or the Prince of Wales come riding by and stopped in front of her she would have been perfectly all right so long as the patrician Dixies had been at her side. They knew the rules.

Once, when she was thirty or so Nell was invited to meet V. in London to witness the marriage procession of the Duke and Duchess of Kent. She and V. arrived early upon the Embankment and took up positions in the front row. Nell carried a little flag to wave hurray. V. in her threadbare coat of ancient design simply stood, but as the carriages came by it

14

seemed the merest accident that V. was on the pavement and not bowing and twirling her wrist from the inside of one of them. "Such a pity about the hat," she said. "The Queen knows never to wear a big hat. She knows that we all want to see her face. Poor Marina of course is Greek," and she led Nell off to a Lyons tea-shop for a little something. V. had to eat a little something every three hours, otherwise she fainted. "Oh poor V.", said plump Nell, "And you're so terribly thin."

"All Dixies are thin."

"But you are really *frighteningly* thin," said Nell, "I do hope you've seen someone."

"Oh, dear me yes. I've seen half a dozen. The girls took me to Harley Street."

"That must have cost – ," said Nell before remembering that prices are never mentioned. "And what did they say?"

"They said," said V. looking across the small sandwiches, "They said I was to eat something every three hours."

"But couldn't you eat *more*?" asked Nell who after twenty-four hours in May's bed-sitting room (which had turned out to be a very nice flat with three bedrooms but a kitchen with only a kettle) was famished. "Couldn't I – well, wouldn't you let me buy you something substantial? Some baked beans?"

V.'s narrow, birdish, sweet face for a moment almost lost its stiff upper lip. "I'm afraid there's no hope of *beans*," she said and went on to discuss train time-tables back to Kent and her mid-week ticket which must not be wasted. She said that there was just time to see a film about Henry VIII that was on at Victoria.

During the bed scene with Anne Boleyn, V. had to leave as she felt a faint coming on, and they went to find a little something in the railway buffet. Nell went to Kings Cross and ate seven sausages and felt disgraceful. As soon as she got home to Leeds she sat down at once to thank for the wonderful outing.

"Particularly the film," she wrote and paused. V. had pronounced the film shocking. "So realistic," she wrote with delighted malice.

"Laughing?" asked the cobbler.

"Oh no," said Nell ashamed, "I'm very fond of V. She's so poor you know. It's just as well she's a Dixie."

"I'd have thought you'd have got all said you wanted, down in London."

The cobbler was a heavy man who sat slumped with a pipe and would never put a bit of coal on the fire or draw a curtain, but he was splendid in bed which had been a glorious surprise to Nell who had expected something unpleasant or just to be endured. Her one experience of sex before marriage had been a fumbling on a landing with Major Dixie in Pickering when she was twelve, an experience she had shared with the governess had she known it (Mrs Dixie had) and with many others. Her marriage, her female self, she never dreamed of even hinting at in her letters to V. and was delighted and surprised by her confident knowledge that she should not. She had mastered an area of etiquette that would never be demanded of the Dixie girls. And much else unknown to the Dixie girls.

At this time, and it was the first time, she began to find it difficult to provide material for letters to V. about sickness and death. It was a relief when the baby came and she could announce nappy rash and gripes and the possibility of infantile thrush, even though V. replied imprecisely about these, countering them, fielding them, with her own familiar symptoms, bravely borne.

So the years passed and everyone grew old and Nell's husband died and Hilda grew to be a large, angry sort of woman very high up in local government. When Nell was eighty-four Hilda retired and they went to live at a sea-side place where Hilda had had meaningful holidays during the menopause with a woman called Audrey, now dead. She took up residence on a pink housing-estate set out in crescents on the ugly edge of a pretty mediaeval town. Gulls screamed, you could hear the waves on rough days and there was a sea-light sometimes in the sky and wide sunsets, but all you could see from the windows were identical windows opposite, very nicely painted, grass well-cut and a shaped hedge.

It was an elderly crescent. Few children played. Nobody much passed by. Nell had one side of a twin-pack semi-det, Hilda the other, an excellent scheme. "I can hear her if she knocks through the wall," said Hilda, "And she's not incontinent yet." Nell was grateful in her way and always waved as Hilda went charging down the next-door path each morning to her clean and glittering little car. Hilda, though retired from London was becoming politically indispensable to the South-East coast. She shopped and cooked for her mother, bursting in each evening with supper from the microwave under a plastic dome. Sometimes on Sundays they ate lunch together. Nell often now called it Sunday dinner in the old way and in the old Yorkshire voice that had reasserted itself as had some nice old words she wondered at even as she spoke them. Her fitted, hot and cold bathroom basin for example had become "the wash-stand" and the dustman's crunching-lorry had become a "dray".

When Nell had become ill with bronchial pneumonia one winter there had been a day when Hilda had stayed home from work to see the doctor who had suggested that now, or at least during the winter months, might not Nell move in with her daughter, but Hilda had said "Now about that I have to be *very* firm. No choices. To be happy and secure, old people must have no choices," and the doctor, humbled, had gone away. He called on Nell once unexpectedly and found her writing letters in a chair by the window. "Oh, very thankful," she said, "Everybody's very kind. I do just wish there was somebody in the day-time and the view is rather poor."

Outings were suggested. Minibuses filled with doleful invalids arrived at the door. The invalids looked out at Nell on the step with little enthusiasm and Nell said to the woman in authority who was trying to lure her towards them that after all she didn't feel up to it. "I get these little faints," she said in a Dixie voice and went in and shut the door and despised herself. "Your mother needs mental stimulation," the authorities told Hilda.

So one day when it was extremely dark and wet, dark and wet as it can only be in sea-side Kent in winter, and when Hilda had no committees, she put her mother in the car and took her for a drive. They sizzled along the sea-front, wind-screen wipers going a-lick, lorries flinging spray all over them and the wind banging. Somewhere along the road beside the invisible white cliffs of Dover Nell said it reminded her of Pickering.

"Pickering?" said Hilda, "Pickering's in the middle of moors."

"Oh, it's quite near the sea."

"Don't be ridiculous."

"I like the East coast. Pickering's North East. I'm glad you brought me East again, Hilda. It's better than London."

"I can't see you in London."

"I've been down here before you know. V. lived down here for years. Vi and May moved down to join her. They all lived somewhere down here at the end."

"Are they all dead now, those women?"

"I got out of touch," said Nell, "After V. died."

"Awful snobs. I couldn't bear them," said Hilda.

"I liked V." said Nell and found herself weeping. The tears wetted her round cheeks. She thought of the schoolroom in snow-light, the golden serrip and the Duchess of Kent. "V. was the last person to write me a letter every week," said Nell, "It's a sad thing when there's nobody to write you a weekly letter."

"Nobody writes me a weekly letter," said Hilda.

"That's because I live with you. I'd be writing to you if I didn't."

18

Hilda remained unmoved by this information.

"I have to think to find people to write to now," said Nell, "It's people's children I write to now, and some of them are getting old. I miss V."

"Was she the one who was always having little rests? Frustrated spinster?" A container truck from Belgium bore down on Hilda's car and tried to fling it into the sea but she stuck to the wheel and held her course, thrusting upward her jaw. "Those women needed a good analyst. Idle. Depressed. We're almost there. I'm not sure it's not too wet to get out."

They were visiting Walmer castle where the Duke of Wellington had breathed his last. It was one pound fifty, seventy-five p. for old-age pensioners and open until six o'clock. Both Nell and Hilda were old-age pensioners so that it was a cheap outing, and also there were few steps, which suited Hilda who had a hip. The gloom of the afternoon had turned to the dark of evening for it was after five o'clock. The rain fell.

Hilda let her mother, whose hips were in order, unlatch herself from her seat-belt and watched her walk light-footed to the ticket-office inside the dark stone keep. Then she went to the car-park, for the tickets were to be her mother's treat.

The ticket-collector looked surprised to see Nell. There was no sign of other visitors. "What weather," said Nell, but he turned his shoulder from her and went on reading the *East Kent Mercury*. Nell went to wait for Hilda on the half-landing of the shallow staircase between the portraits of Wellington and Napoleon after Waterloo. "Such a proud nose, Wellington's," thought Nell, "So strained you can almost see the bone shining through. It's a bit like Major Dixie's." She turned to Napoleon who was surveying the world that had bowled him over the cliff. The pale, pale face. The wisps of blown scant hair. The plebeian neck. Too big a hat, like Marina of Kent. The eyes burned with the desolation of the eternal dark. Hilda coming up, dot and carry, said it

19

was an upsetting picture.

They walked along a cold corridor in to the Duke of Wellington's death chamber where the shabby chair he died in stood untouched since he had last sat in it. Near it stood his iron camp-bed with its single dreary blanket. "It's very austere," said Nell, "Of course, that's the Army." Standing in the greenish shadow of the window alcove was a woman, lean, shoulderless, colourless, in faded clothes. She seemed to be part of the texture of the scoured grey wall behind her. Nell thought, "It's V. She is not dead," but as the woman came forward she saw that it was only May.

They stared at each other for a moment and then May said, "Why, it's little bread and serrip. I thought you were gone long ago Nell."

They walked together round the Duke's apartments. They examined the furniture that had belonged to an assortment of the great – William Pitt, Lord Byron. "It's rather damp here," said Nell, "It needs some warmth to put the bloom back in it, and a warmed wax polish."

May said that Queen Victoria and all her children had used the castle for sea-side holidays. "Just think," she said, "All the little crinolines swinging about." Conversation waned.

"I expect there's central-heating now," said May. "In the State apartments. Where the Queen Mother stays. She often comes here you know. But then, she's used to draughts in Scotland."

"I'm sure they must have done something about a radiator for the Queen Mother," said Nell.

"Of course the Duke had no need of it," said May, "The Army doesn't hear of it."

"Well, I do," said Hilda, "And I think we should be hurrying up."

The two old women went out by the draw-bridge, Hilda limping behind. "I'll write," said Nell, "It has been wonderful. When did –? Did Vi –?"

"Vi went seven years ago. Two years after V."

20

"Time goes," said Nell, "I'll write. You have my address? We're in the book."

"Goodbye," they all said, "Goodbye," and left May in the dark rain looking autocratically about for a taxi.

As Nell had forgotten to ask May for her address, nothing came of this meeting. No telephone call came to the crescent and Nell found that somehow she didn't want to look up May's address. Hilda forgot. In the Spring, though, another outing took place and as Nell and her daughter flew between the tall trees and the sea near St Margaret's Bay Nell said, waking from some dream, "The Dixies. They used to live here. This is where I stayed with V. and Vi. Oh – in the forties. Oh, I could take you straight to the house."

"Well, all right. Something to do," said Hilda swinging seawards, missing a cat. Up and round the sandy curving road they went, past good houses in wide blowy gardens. "It reminded them all of Brittany," said Nell, "One year the Major took them all to Brittany. It was before tourists." She felt proud to have known people who knew where to go abroad without being told. "Not many knew Brittany before the War," she said.

"I suppose the Bretons did," said Hilda, "I don't know why you're so in love with those Dixies."

"Not in love," said Nell, "I don't know what it is. Here. Up here," she said, "That court-yard."

And so it was. "You've still a memory," said Hilda accusingly, "But you'd better take a grip I'm afraid, Mother, because you're going to be disappointed. I *very* much fear," and she crashed the brakes and hobbled from the car to ring a door-bell with authority. She gazed about her as if the court-yard needed dealing with, which it did not.

The door opened, Nell saw, on pine walls, an Aga cooker, dried herbs in bunches, a wine-rack and a girl who looked fourteen with a baby under her arm and a tail of hair swinging cheerfully about behind her as she turned to look for an address. Music and a smell of garlic and warmth floated out

21

towards Hilda's car.

"Moved," said Hilda, returning, buckling herself in, "Four months ago. Can't find the forwarding address but it's a nursing-home down the road. She described it. Not far from the castle. D'you want to go and find it?"

Nell, surprised by choice said yes, she did and looked sideways at Hilda's strong profile, grateful. "After all, nothing else to do," said Hilda, "Unless we go back for another look at Wellington's death-chamber. Shouldn't take long."

But there were several candidates for May Dixie's latest resting place. At least six large, gable-ended houses that could only be nursing-homes flanked the castle and the sea. Hilda disappeared inside the huge unlocked front door of one of them, a grey-green flaking edifice with shutters drawn across many windows and heavy net obscuring others. Nell sat in the car in the silent circular drive. In one window stood three drooping peacock feathers. From another a white, monkey-face peeped. Nell looked at the empty flower-beds.

After some time Hilda returned, looking shaken. "No reply," she said, "Nobody there."

"Nobody?"

"Knocked on five doors. Great big doors. Golf-clubs in the hall – awful, sandy-looking old tiles. Golf-clubs had spiders' webs in them. Everything silent but after you'd knocked it grew more silent. Listened at one door first and there was a – medical sort of voice. I knocked and it stopped. You could smell the hypodermics. And that other smell. That rich, geriatric smell."

"I don't like a poor geriatric smell," said Nell who had once lately been in a public geriatric ward, "It doesn't sound like the Dixies. I didn't know you had such a fancy, Hilda."

"You're never to go to a place like that, Ma, never," and Nell in sudden joy looked at her with love and said she didn't intend to and thank goodness she had no money. "I wouldn't mind a nice State home though, where you all sit round nodding off or watch the telly. And you get your meals brought on trays. And all the respectable ones change their characters and start swearing."

Hilda rolled the usual hostile glance.

"And you all wear old bits, and have nips of sherry."

"I don't know what you're talking about," said Hilda, "God help us all at the end, that's all. All I hope is that I go fast and soon."

"Oh, not too soon," said Nell, "Not too fast."

"Couldn't be too fast for me," said Hilda, "Here, what's this one? This looks more like Dixies."

A very spruce, large house on a corner, newly-decorated in rich deep cream which showed off the red brick, stood before them. A brass plate announced The Grove and beneath it a brown plate added "Retirement Home. No tradesmen." Along all the pretty french windows on the ground floor only the top of one white hospital screen was sinister. Polished fat bulbs were coming up in all the borders and on one of the balconies upstairs, facing the sea, there already stood a summer basket chair. "I remember that chair," said Nell.

Hilda marched up the path and a smiling, very clean young man with a gold earring and holding a bright orange duster answered the door. There were two or three moments of intense conversation and Hilda came back and sat firmly and sensibly behind the wheel again. "Bad news," she said, "I'm afraid, Mother. Bad news. She's only just died. About a month ago."

"So odd," said Nell, "Coming to the door with a duster. She wouldn't have liked that."

"They're very upset," said Hilda. In her new vulnerability after the cobwebbed golf-clubs, the whispering demon doctors, she looked warily towards her mother to see how she had taken it.

"D'you know, I *thought* she might be dead," said Nell, "Somehow I had a feeling. I never really liked May. She had a

23

mean little face when you come to think about it."

They drove more slowly away. "She didn't die there," said Hilda, "Not at The Grange. They'd had her temporarily moved while they were being re-decorated. They sounded genuinely upset. That man said she was one of the old school. Proud she was going to go through with something. The young man said it had been a big shock to them."

"Well, it would be," said Nell, "Very expensive those places. It must be quite difficult to fill them up. I wonder if she took the old furniture. I expect she left them that chair. I wonder who got the rest? I never really liked May."

"But a nice young man," said Hilda and thought, there's something queer here: I'm beginning to talk like her and she like me.

"Diamonds in his ears," said Nell, "There's a lot of that about. I'd not have thought May would have cared for it. I wonder why she died."

"Shock. Heart. Being moved at that time of life. Too old for hotels."

"I've always had a fancy for hotels," said Nell, "I never stayed in one."

"The Grand Duke," said Hilda, "Good Lord – there it is."

"That!" said Nell. It was a tall slit of a building painted purple with dark red curtains and dirty brass rails across the inside of the windows, which were grimy. A tremendous noise of shouting and bleeping, the booming of fruit-machines and a general din of youth issued from within. A second door stood beside the open door of the pub. Painted beside it with an arrow pointed upwards was the word Rooms. Hilda's car had been halted outside this pub on a roundabout solid with traffic en route eastward for France and westward for the Medway towns. They were greatly intertwined. A frightful place. Nell unclicked her seat-belt and got out.

"What in *hell* are you doing," said Hilda, reversing.

"Oh, I must just have a – "

"Get back in the car at once." But behind her the seething lorries bellowed and honked.

"Park, dear, and come back for me," said Nell and vanished inside the pub where she sat down at an iron table in the corner. It was awash with beer. Her feet did not touch the floor. She swung them.

A man came across to her, very fat. The rolls of fat showed through his tee-shirt like the rolls of a brisket of beef. He wiped the table. He had an old-young baby-face. Pouting, he watched the damp cloth moving. Outside, the traffic made the whole of the Grand Duke vibrate. He had to shout above it and above the clashing of the music.

"It's nearly closing time."

"I don't really want – ," said Nell, "My friend died here."

"Not Miss Dixie?" The fat mat sat down, "Oh, my dear! She seemed so comfortable. Such a surprise. It had been her own choice to come you know. You can't blame Gary. Something to do with Wellington. She scarcely spoke. Oh, she was a real old stager. A lady. We took all her meals up."

"Well, she wasn't really my friend, it was her sister," said Nell.

"She had a very old-fashioned voice," said the fat man, "A pleasure to hear her."

"It was the Army," said Nell.

A cheer went up. Somebody had won a fortune. A robot pulsated, spoke from a deep throat. Two young men began to fight on the floor and others to shout and laugh. "That's the Army, too," said the fat man, "The Marines from down the road. When she was here she was on about some Blues and Greys. There's always been soldiers here. But she kept her distance. She'd only known officers. It wasn't what she'd expected."

"I could live here," said Nell, "I could just live here nicely. Could I just get a look at May's room?"

Outside they went and up the steep stairs and inside. The

room seemed all to be covered in delicate grey mole-skin. When you touched it, it moved, for it was dust. "We found her just over there," said the man, "All huddled. Right away from the view. One of the few things she said was that at The Grange you had 'the Duke's view' – whatever that meant." He pointed a toe about on the dusty Turkey carpet. On the carpet, some of them stacked up, were a great many little red and gold chairs and a high knobbly bed. There were dried grasses in jars and great windows at each end of the room. The sea boomed. Nell said, "I could enjoy it here."

"It's the traffic's the problem," said the fat man, "The noise. There's the terrible noise of the roundabout. You can't deny it. Accidents all the time. There's one now. Can you hear it?"

She could and it turned out to have been poor angry Hilda who had gone slap into a tanker and was no more. Nell moved to the pub and became a fixture there in her corner seat, living on for some years. She drank sweet sherry all day long and grew fatter than the landlord, rejoicing in the clamour within and without. The Yorkshire accent was gentle and it flew free. She swung her foot in time to the terrible music.

Sometimes she talked to the soldiers about other soldiers and old wars and of her husband who had never once mentioned the Somme. They asked her what the Somme was, and she was unsure.

"Who is she?" new recruits would ask, "Her in the corner?"

"Don't know. She was one of The Dixie Girls or something."

"What's the Dixie Girls?"

"Don't know. Some old song and dance act. Nobody's ever heard of them."

BENEVOLENCE

"IT's me dad. He's bad."

The boy on the doorstep was about twelve, and fat. Short-legged and square. "He's bad." He pointed into the dark.

He pointed down the Caplan-Fairleys' wide suburban drive, so long that it had an ornamental lamp-post half-way down it, on a bend, to light the rhododendron bushes, heavy with snow. New snow was beginning to fall on the fat boy and Milo held the door wider to say come in: then, seeing the boy's eyes, instead he said, "Where?"

Without a coat he ran after the boy down the drive, past the lamp-post and at length to the gates, their four feet making a galloping track in the thick, frosted gravel.

A man lay in the gutter. Despite the rural appearance of the Caplan-Fairleys' drive there was a gutter at the end of it and a yellow line, for in the daytime the road was a favourite rush-hour loop-through to the City, ten miles away. Yet now, at night, the house heard scarcely a whisper of traffic.

It was called *Trelawn*, one of a few huge houses standing along a ridge, their gardens sweeping down to the yellow line and spreading amply to either side. The houses were at a greater than geographical distance from each other, garden-wall or parish-pump behaviour being what their owners had moved there to escape. "You can get away from people here," they said. "After London it's wonderful." At summer-evening parties guests said to each other that they might really be in the country. In winter the houses were constantly burgled.

The Caplan-Fairleys loved *Trelawn* and used it to the full. From their youth – their very rich youth: they had always been rich – they had been blessed with a powerful feeling for

27

those less fortunate than themselves. Their first home had been a Knightsbridge apartment where they were younger by a generation than anyone else in the block. Their thick, shocking-pink carpets and gilt and crystal chandeliers had quite stunned friends who had known them only as Sociology students at Birmingham and not quite understood the reasons for their great self-confidence. College accommodation is a great masker of taste.

In the Knightsbridge days the old chums would be invited for little snacks to show what homely souls the Caplan-Fairleys really were. "We pig it," said Fay, "We hardly *use* the dining-room," and served little blackberry mounds of caviare and frail rolls of Harrods Parma ham at the marble kitchen table.

Always the Caplan-Fairleys had been dogged, torn between their feeling of affectionate equality with the poor and the need to display their own apparently effortless prosperity.

And oh, they were kind. They would lend you anything – their house, their car, their children's nannie – when they were out of the country and not needing them. They would lend them even if you were not needing them either. If you were going to a party Fay would be round with the best of her heavy jewellery for you to wear. If you were giving a party Rowland saw to it that his most expensive pot-plants were delivered for the evening, though they dwarfed and made listless your just-arranged flowers. When they took you to Glyndebourne – they took less well-heeled friends several times a season even though they themselves were not musical and sat glazed throughout what they called "the show" – when they took you to Glyndebourne – it never rained, nobody ever sat in the butter, their hamper was the biggest and best of any on the lawns and their champagne wrapped in the most dazzling napkin. Fay would always ring up a day or two before, to see if she could help you with the appropriate clothes, and afterwards, when you parted from them in the pale dawn, their eyes would meet yours and tell you that they thought absolutely no less of you because you were unused to such perfection. Wonderful hosts, the Caplan-Fairleys. Unenthusiastic guests.

They expected complete loyalty of course. You had to abandon private plans. Everything had to be dropped to take up last-minute theatre-seats when some business guest fell out. ("And look, don't feel you *have* to come on with us to the Savoy afterwards"). Similarly, if an important business client were to become available after all, you would be expected to give up the seats without demur. There was nobody who could give you a better time than the Caplan-Fairleys so long as you agreed without word or sign to cede all your territory: to accept the image that they had of you, and circulated about you, and never complain or present arguments or ideas of any kind. If you strayed towards an argument or idea the Caplan-Fairleys would look grave. They had no religious interest, no politics, no sense of history. Greece and Italy were a matter of hotels to them. Egypt a great place for racing. The Orient was a poor place for golf-courses and India, of course unvisitable. Yet they were good people, giving much to charity and good works. Much time and much money.

They looked wonderful. Fay wore bright clothes, often white. A good deal of cashmere, hung with gold chains. Her nails seemed always just to have been done, her hair that moment sculpted, her face enamelled like a mask. She was always scented and like an American her clothes seemed always new. She seemed always to have just reached the age that suited her best.

Rowland wore suits of enormous price, perhaps a little tight across the chest, again in a slightly transatlantic way, and also looking new – so new that you imagined they must be off the peg, until you saw the wonderful hand-stitching. And beneath the hand-stitching the chest was strong and broad, bronzed like his face by three good overseas holidays a year.

He was relaxed, unhurried, secure – the managing director of his family firm which now was backed by foreign money. He ran his bosses with an overlordly good nature and never slipped up on an employee's name.

But it was their children who were their greatest marvels. There were three. Sons. And not one of them had ever put a foot wrong in his life. The eldest was a barrister, very fashionable but very sound. He ran a Boys' Club in Brixton, boasted black friends yet was a member of the Garrick. The second was in his father's firm and doing splendidly. He was an earnest magistrate and promising skier, tipped for the British team.

The third was Milo, a late joy, born when Fay was over forty, and now nineteen. Milo still lived at home but would be leaving as soon as his final school examinations were achieved. These were proving tardy, but Fay and Rowland knew that it didn't help to worry about one's children's academic achievements just as they knew they mustn't coddle him for ever.

"We'll throw you out of the nest, won't we Milie darling?"

"Can't wait," said Milo, eating delicious food cooked for him by the cook from silver polished by the housekeeper and wearing a shirt ironed beautifully by his old nannie.

The man lay in the gutter.

Milo wasn't really spoilt. He was a nice boy. Sweet. Amiable. Nobody knew him very well – perhaps there wasn't much to know. He stayed in his room a lot and had few friends. He did no harm to anyone. The Caplan-Fairleys, experienced in social work with the young, recognised the hazards lying ahead for Milo in their parental excellence. They confided, particularly to their working-class friends, that wealth puts a great burden on a child, especially the youngest. So easy to relax one's standards. To dote. One's ewelamb.

So, as he grew up, Milo had been sent on various dangerous and taxing pursuits, like rock-climbing or jumping out of

30

aeroplanes, and on the school expedition to Greenland. When he became an experienced climber he had led parties from his brother's Boys' Club, sometimes with other youth leaders, sometimes alone. No friendships resulted from these outings which made Fay a little troubled. She gave parties for Milo, importing many girls. He smiled a lot at the parties and saw to the music. "He should have slept with someone by now," said Fay, but Rowland wasn't worried. "He's a man," he said, "He knows how to rough it. For God's sake, that last trip to the Alps they had no doors on the loos. They all slept in their socks."

The man lay neatly, almost tucked in along the kerb, his face pressed against the grid of a drain. He was narrow. At first he looked not so much a man as a bundle of shabby clothes that might have fallen from some rubbish cart. A bicycle lay near him and another bike, the boy's, lay abandoned across the pavement, one gawky pedal in the air. The man lay still.

"It's me dad. Me *dad*," the fat boy said again. "He fell off. He wouldn't get off at the hill."

Feet came running down the drive and from the house someone switched on the electric flames on the gate-posts. Rowland, his sheepskin coat flapping, stopped between them. "Don't touch him," he shouted. "Ambulance." But Milo had already flung the fallen bike away and turned the thin bundle over. The gate-lights showed a face glossy with sweat, eyes closed, cheekbones sharp, nose sharper, bared to the snowflakes.

"Kiss of life," said Milo, and the boy gave a whimper.

"Hold on now," said his father. "Steady on." The man's mouth was purple and slack, hanging open a little. He had terrible teeth. Milo fastened his mouth over the man's mouth and blew into it as he had been taught on his First-Aid class before the Jungfrau. He worked steadily on the man, pressing on him, jerking his arms. Rowland ran back to the house and the telephone and returned with Fay who stood regally, her

31

hair protected by a huge gauzy chiffon, silvery with snow. She pressed the fat boy to the side of her mink-lined rain-coat. He had wet himself. Milo worked and Rowland stood. The boy whimpered again.

"Leave it," said the ambulance men. "No go. No good."

Milo fell back on his heels. Soon the bundle, Rowland and the ambulance-men were gone, the red tail-lights dropping quickly from sight down the hill. After a minute, from where the traffic began they heard the siren begin to ripple and bleat. Milo, kneeling in the road, bowed his head into the snow and retched. "Oh God," said his mother. "Oh my God – you'll catch something. Go in. Gargle. Wash. Have a bath. I'll get the car."

"No. I'll come. Where d'you live?" he asked the boy, and put him in the back seat of his car. Fay called a message to someone inside the house, slammed the front door, and got in beside him. "Me bike!" the boy cried out, as they reached the gates. "Me dad's bike. That's a new bike."

"They'll be all right," said Fay. "We've got to tell your mother."

It was fifteen minutes away, a street of anonymous houses with tight-drawn blinds, and before the car had stopped the boy was out and up the path of one of them and beating against its door. There was no light inside but it opened at once. A voice said "Is it trouble? Is it police?"

In the hospital Rowland, Fay, Milo, the fat boy and the mother sat in a row and waited. The mother sat still, jaw set, mouth a line. She did not touch the boy who sat apart at the end of the bench. They did not cry. When someone came to say that the man was dead the woman looked startled and began to fumble furtively in her bag for a cigarette and the boy ran out of the hospital into the night.

It took Milo some time to find him and to unhook his hands from the rail fencing off the hospital dustbins. He brought the boy back silently and at length relatives came and stood in a bunch over by the door, hesitant and perplexed, as if trying to

32

remember some old book of rules. At last, uncertainly, they took mother and son away and when Rowland had had a magisterial word with the doctors, the Caplan-Fairleys also went home. Milo stopped off at the gates of *Trelawn* to pick up the bikes. He wheeled them up the drive side by side and without saying goodnight went up to bed and was sick in the bathroom. Fay in the master-suite of the house lay cold in her husband's arms.

After a time Rowland said:

"Heart, poor bugger. Out of work. Second attack. He was thirty-two."

"Why us? Oh Rowland – why at our door?"

"Where better?" he said.

He lay heavily, imperially, planning what must next be done.

First came the funeral and the cremation. These Rowland organised and the whole Caplan-Fairley family attended. After it he drove the widow and boy home and took away papers and found a solicitor. The next day he spent a long session in the scruffy house trying to discover the widow's income, which seemed to be nil. "There's the Sup Ben," she said, "That's all. It was 'is heart, see? He couldn't work."

Then Fay took over, sitting every morning in the airless house as the widow smoked and looked at the fireplace. The widow never questioned any of these visits and seemed neither pleased nor sorry when the Caplan-Fairleys arrived, neither pleased nor sorry when they left. They left her alone – except for their telephone number – for a week.

On the eighth day she rang up and, after a silence, said she wanted to see Milo. She had a present for him. He visited her and was given two magnificent video recorders.

"Two?" said Milo.

"They're good quality," said the widow. "They're both the same."

"She's given me two videos," said Milo. "The best."

"Oh, there's no real lack of money there," said Rowland.

"They have everything. I dare say he had a good job before he was ill. They have stereos, microwaves. The boy has a computer. It's their mental security that's damaged. It's the physical shock. They'll come through, but they'll have to be cushioned. It's a great step – giving you these things. They're learning to give."

"It's funny," said Milo. "Two."

"Most interesting psychologically," said Fay. "And rather touching."

"Or maybe," said Milo, "the man was in videos."

"He wasn't in anything."

"He might have been in bikes. That's an impressive bike. They're both good. What do we do with them? It'll be upsetting for her if we take them back. I suppose we'd better ask her."

The widow did not want the bikes back. The boy had gone off his and the widow said she couldn't abide the sight of her husband's. They could sell them if they liked. She didn't want to know.

"I'm not sure that we know how to sell bikes," said Fay, "but we'll try."

"Keep them," said the widow, lighting a new cigarette from a stump; and in the end the barrister son took them for his Boys' Club and found an old sliced loaf and some rancid butter in the saddle-bag of the dead man. He wondered why they had been riding with such things through the night.

"It would be their supper," said Rowland. "Poor things."

"Why were they riding up the ridge anyway?" asked his son. "Did we ever find out?"

"She said it was for his health. To get exercise. And to get the boy's weight down."

"We ought to leave them on their own for a bit now," said Milo unexpectedly.

"So long as they know that we are always here," said Fay.

The very next day the widow rang to say that she needed help in selling a car. It had to go, she said. There was no one to drive it. She had to have the money and there was a garage that would take it but no one to take it to the garage.

"Could the garage not come to you?" asked Fay, professionally watching for danger-signals of over-dependence.

"No," said the widow.

"We'll send down our chauffeur."

"The mister'd get a better price."

"I don't think my husband has ever sold a car himself."

"But it'd look better," said the widow.

So Milo and Rowland drove down in the Porsche, picked up the dead man's car and proceeded in convoy to the garage. The proprietor looked sharply at them, walked round it, kicked it here and there and gave a glance at the engine. He named a price which Rowland agreed.

"You might as well take this back with you," said the garage proprietor, lifting a crowbar out of the boot.

"How odd," said Rowland, "I've really no use for a crowbar and I'm sure the widow hasn't. I'm sure you could have it."

"No thanks," he said, and "No thanks," said the widow when it was offered to her.

"We are the owners of a crowbar," said Rowland to Fay and propped it in the porch. "A talisman," he said. "Videos, bicycles, crowbars. Three triumphs. And she isn't from the present-giving class. This is a considerable gesture. I wonder why they owned a crowbar?"

A week later the widow telephoned again. She asked to speak to the mister and then fell silent. At last she said, coughing, that the Council would be coming after the house now, and put down the telephone. Rowland, driving to see her found her sitting by the stairs on a broken chair regarding the wall. The boy was in the sitting-room eating Chinese take-away on an upturned box and watching the testcard on the television set. He had not been at school for a week. All the furniture had disappeared. The next day Fay installed them both in the chauffeur's flat over one of the *Trelawn* garages for they had recently bought the chauffeur his own house half-way up the ridge and nothing could have been more convenient. Widow and son melted into the flat like beetles into a wainscot and a new phase of everyone's life began.

At first they seemed bewildered, even frightened. The boy was almost invisible and seen only occasionally, slipping around the rhododendrons on his way to the school bus. He and his mother ate Sunday lunch with the Caplan-Fairleys every week – it was a point of principle, said Rowland, and they must attend whoever else was invited. The two sat quietly, looking at their plates, side by side, at the end of the table nearest the kitchen. Other guests sometimes found them rather unnerving, the widow hunched in her chair, smoking between courses, her eyes flickering in what might have been fear or even malevolence.

During the week it was her duty to be about the house – to help with cooking, preparing vegetables, and cleaning and Fay would come down to her pretty desk between kitchen and breakfast-room each morning to direct the day, and look her over. Usually the widow seemed just to be sitting, cigarette in yellow hand, cloth and polish neglected before her, eyes fixed on the kitchen television set. A little darkness seemed to go about with her. She was like a smudge in the gleaming rooms. Even the dog went a long way round rather than pass her chair.

"I'd estimate three months," said Rowland. "Three months before she is over the shock," and Fay agreed. They treated the widow with refreshing brightness, never over-hearty, never cloying. Rowland often put an avuncular hand on her shoulder after setting down in front of her the evening gin and tonic. The widow sat.

"But the boy never speaks at all," said Fay. "The mother is silent but the child might be clinically dumb."

"He's like a rat," said Milo, who never spoke ill, "A fat rat. He slopes off to school at daybreak. Leaving the sinking ship. Or as if he's just planted a bomb."

"But very brave," said Rowland. "He passes the place where it happened twice a day, poor lad. He's going to need a lot of care over the next months."

"He's fairly dreadful. So's his mother when it comes down to it."

Rowland looked gravely at his son.

Yet Milo was fascinated by the pair. He watched them. And he watched them watching him. He felt the boy's knowledge that he was being watched, and his disregard for it. He felt himself mysteriously threatened and found this fascinating, too. "If you don't mind my saying so," he said one day to his parents, "We are being made mugs of."

But the Caplan-Fairleys did mind, and when the housekeeper and then the nannie began to say the same, they minded more. Rowland gave the widow a bigger cheque for Christmas than he had intended and Fay bought them on impulse some warmer curtains. "Christmas Day?" said Rowland. "Of course they'll be here on Christmas Day. Where else can they go? The relations have disappeared."

"We are making a mistake," said Milo.

"Duty is never mistaken," said Rowland. When the widow turned up at the Christmas dinner bearing a present for Rowland of a brass-gold watch set with diamonds and a strap like a wattle fence – "Something he got given" – Rowland was delighted and said so. The widow lit another cigarette.

In the New Year Honours Rowland received the OBE: for his long career in good works and public service and it was also his thirtieth wedding anniversary and the excuse for an enormous party. This was attended by almost everyone he and Fay had ever known, including a scattering of people in positions of authority. They mixed democratically though somehow not easily among the usual host of the deprived and the unfortunate. There was a bishop, a judge, a couple of politicians whose faces you felt you ought to know, a Liberal peer and a fashionable psychologist. Rowland was everywhere, moving people about. "Must split up the eggheads," he cried pushing between the bishop and a Fellow of All Souls with a very bright girl who was his wife's hairdresser. Sweaty with champagne, he cried to the psychologist, "And here's the widow. Our very own widow. Husband died at our door. Great friend of all of us. Lives with us. Our boy takes her boy rock-climbing, don't you Milie?"

The widow sat darkly in the middle of the party, chin in hand. "Good evening," said the psychologist without enthusiasm. The widow scratched her head which had not been washed for the party. The psychologist felt his work was following him about. Rowland put an arm round the widow's unappetising shoulders and shouted, "You could take our widow anywhere." And Milo hearing these dreadful words saw that the boy was looking at his father with quintessential hatred.

A moment later, feeling Milo's eyes on him, the boy turned and looked Milo full in the face and the look of loathing stayed steady. Fay came forward and began to heap the widow's plate.

The following day, a Sunday, an icy, foggy day, Milo was to take the boy rock-climbing in Kent. They had been together several times before but in better weather and although the boy was beginning to climb rather well, he was nervous. They were to do a new climb today, rated "difficult/severe". The boy had received the news of the outing with his usual, unmoving face.

But as Milo approached the door of the flat over the garage in the early morning he heard a new tune. Mother and son were engaged in raucous and screaming fury. . . "bloody well staying home," yelled the boy. ". . . bloody well going and watch yourself or it's all over," shrieked the widow. Milo stood for a long time on the step before ringing the bell. At length the boy came out.

Two hours later at the top of the climb Milo took in rope for the boy who hung some twenty feet below him, with a hundred feet below that. Milo fastened the rope twice round himself and left all the long length of slack below. Milo then sat down on the cliff-top, and there was silence in the frosty morning.

The boy hung, swinging slightly. "Hey?" he shouted at last.

Milo sat on.

"Milo?" shouted the boy, "Hey?"

Silence.

"Milo? Hey. I'm stopped. Milo?"

He began to kick about on the rock, scrabbling his feet. He heaved on his arms and his feet slid beneath him. The rock was slippery. The loose rope had begun to swing.

"Milo! Don't let go."

At last Milo said – it was so still that he had hardly to raise his voice, hardly to lean forward – "So, what was the bread for?"

A deeper silence fell upon the cliff and the boy did nothing. In time Milo gave himself a heave and hauled in the rope, and after a time the head and shoulders of the boy appeared at the rock's edge. The two said nothing to each other.

They said nothing to each other for an hour of the journey home and then Milo stopped the car on the hard shoulder, just short of the tunnel into London and looked straight ahead of him and waited.

"You stick it on the glass," said the boy, "With butter and that. You don't hear the breaking glass."

"Did you do it or just your father?"

"He did the break-ins. When I was little, he pushed me in, though."

"Was he going to push you in a house on our ridge? Into our house?"

"Somewhere. Being fat I wasn't so good as I'd been. He'd been mad at me, getting fat."

He looked at Milo, "He'd not know me now. Thinner with the climbing and that."

"Was your father good? Good at it?"

"What – at thieving? Yes, he was good."

Milo re-started the car and drove home fast. The boy said, "He was good all right. That quiet. He was the best, me dad."

"Did he ever get caught?"

"Oh he'd been caught. He'd done time."

"Did you mind? Going out with him?"

"No. He was dead good."

"So you miss it? Your dad, and thieving?"

"I miss thieving. I don't miss me dad. Not now. He'd gone nervous."

"What's good about thieving?"

"It's exciting. Gives yer a thrill. Gives yer a buzz."

"Taking people's things?"

"It's not people. It's not against people. It's just it's great."

"So life's not what it was?"

"It's all right. It's just it's boring."

"You don't want to change then? Be like – well have the life I've got?"

"I wouldn't want the life you've got."

"My parents are good people. Loving people."

The boy said nothing until they turned in between *Trelawn's* great imitation torches.

"Why don't you and me go out?" said the boy, "You'd like it. You'd be dead good."

"Good day?" called Fay across the parquet. Her face shone with pride at the sight of Milo walking into the hall. So straight, so handsome, so fine and rosy from the bright hard weather. His massive climbing rope coiled over his shoulder was like the armour of a knight. "How did the boy get on?"

"Very well."

"We'll make something of him. You'll see. *You*'ll make something of him, darling Milie. I know you will. Just see."

"Could you leave it, Ma?"

40

"Leave it? My darling – "

"Oh leave it, can't you? Can't you grow up?"

Unruffled still, Fay said, "But you will? You won't drop him? You will go out with him again, won't you?"

"I might," said Milo. He flung the hard filthy rope across the shining floor, "I might," he said. "You never know."

BANG, BANG – WHO'S DEAD?

THERE is an old house in Kent not far from the sea where a little ghost girl plays in the garden. She wears the same clothes winter and summer – long black stockings, a white dress with a pinafore, and her hair flying about without a hat, but she never seems either hot or cold. They say she was a child of the house who was run over at the drive gates, for the road outside is on an upward bend as you come to the gates of The Elms – that's the name of the house, The Elms – and very dangerous. But there were no motor cars when children wore clothes like that and so the story must be rubbish.

No grown person has even seen the child. Only other children see her. For over fifty years, when children have visited this garden and gone off to play in it, down the avenue of trees, into the walled rose-garden, or down deep under the high dark caves of the polished shrubs where queer things scutter and scrattle about on quick legs and eyes look out at you from round corners, and pheasants send up great alarm calls like rattles, and whirr off out of the wet hard bracken right under your nose, "Where've you been?" they get asked when they get back to the house.

"Playing with that girl in the garden."

"What girl? There's no girl here. This house has no children in it."

"Yes it has. There's a girl in the garden. She can't half run."

When last year The Elms came up for sale, two parents – the parents of a girl called Fran – looked at each other with a great longing gaze. The Elms.

"We could never afford it."

"I don't know. It's in poor condition. We might. They

43

daren't ask much for such an overgrown place."

"All that garden. We'd never be able to manage it. And the house is so far from anywhere."

"It's mostly woodland. It looks after itself."

"Don't you believe it. Those elms would all have to come down for a start. They're diseased. There's masses of re-planting and clearing to do. And think of the upkeep of that long drive."

"It's a beautiful house. And not really a huge one."

"And would you *want* to live in a house with – "

They both looked at Fran who had never heard of the house. "With what?" she asked.

"Is it haunted?" she asked. She knew things before you ever said them. Almost before you thought of them.

"Of course not," said her father.

"Yes," said her mother.

Fran gave a squealing shudder.

"Now you've done it," said her father. "No point now in even going to look at it."

"How is it haunted?" asked Fran.

"It's only the garden," said her mother. "And very *nicely* haunted. By a girl about your age in black stockings and a pinafore."

"What's a pinafore?"

"Apron."

"*Apron.* How cruddy."

"She's from the olden days."

"Fuddy-duddy-cruddy," said Fran, preening herself about in her tee-shirt and jeans.

After a while though she noticed that her parents were still rattling on about The Elms. There would be spurts of talks and then long silences. They would stand for ages moving things pointlessly about on the kitchen table, drying up the same plate three times. Gazing out of windows. In the middle of Fran telling them something about her life at school they would say suddenly, "Rats. I expect it's overrun with rats."

Or, "What about the roof?"

Or, "I expect some millionaire will buy it for a Country Club. Oh, it's far beyond us, you know."

"When are we going to look at it?" asked Fran after several days of this, and both parents turned to her with faraway eyes.

"I want to see this girl in the garden," said Fran because it was a bright sunny morning and the radio was playing loud and children not of the olden days were in the street outside, hurling themselves about on bikes and wearing jeans and tee-shirts like her own and shouting out, "Bang, bang, you're dead."

"Well, I suppose we could just telephone," said her mother. "Make an appointment."

Then electricity went flying about the kitchen and her father began to sing.

They stopped the car for a moment inside the propped-back iron gates where there stood a rickety table with a box on it labelled "Entrance Fee. One pound."

"We don't pay an entrance fee," said Fran's father. "We're here on business."

"When I came here as a child," said Fran's mother, "We always threw some money in."

"Did you often come?"

"Oh, once or twice. Well yes. Quite often. Whenever we had visitors we always brought them to The Elms. We used to tell them about – "

"Oh yes. Ha-ha. The ghost."

"Well, it was just something to do with people. On a visit. I'd not be surprised if the people in the house made up the ghost just to get people to come."

The car ground along the silent drive. The drive curved round and round. Along and along. A young deer leapt from one side of it to the other in the green shadow, its eyes like lighted grapes. Water in a pool in front of the house came into

45

view.

The house held light from the water. It was a long, low, creamy-coloured house covered with trellis and on the trellis pale wisteria, pale clematis, large papery early roses. A huge man was staring from the gound-floor window.

"Is that the ghost?" asked Fran.

Her father sagely, solemnly parked the car. The air in the garden for a moment seemed to stir, the colours to fade. Fran's mother looked up at the gentle old house.

"Oh – look," she said, "It's a portrait. Of a man. He seems to be looking out. It's just a painting, for goodness sake."

But the face of the long-dead seventeenth-century man eyed the terrace, the semi-circular flight of steps, the family of three looking up at him beside their motor-car.

"It's just a painting."

"Do we ring the bell? At the front door?"

The half-glazed inner front door above the staircase of stone seemed the door of another shadowy world.

"I don't want to go in," said Fran. "I'll stay here."

"Look, if we're going to buy this house," said her father, "You must come and look at it."

"I want to go in the garden," said Fran. "Anyone can see the house is going to be all right."

All three surveyed the pretty house. Along the top floor of it were heavily-barred windows.

"They barred the windows long ago," said Fran's mother, "To stop the children falling out. The children lived upstairs. Every evening they were allowed to come down and see their parents for half an hour and then they went back up there to bed. It was the custom for children."

"Did the ghost girl do that?"

"Don't be ridiculous," said Fran's father.

"But did she?"

"What ghost girl?" said Fran's father. "Shut up and come and let's look at the house."

*   *   *

46

A man and a woman were standing at the end of the hall as the family rang the bell. They were there waiting, looking rather vague and thin. Fran could feel a sadness and anxiety through the glass of the wide, high door, the woman with her gaunt old face just standing; the man blinking.

In the beautiful stone hall at the foot of the stairs the owners and the parents and Fran confronted each other. Then the four grown people advanced with their hands outstretched, like some dance.

"The house has always been in my family," said the woman. "For two hundred years."

"Can I go out?" asked Fran.

"For over fifty years it was in the possession of three sisters. My three great-aunts."

"Mum – can I? I'll stay by the car."

"They never married. They adored the house. They scarcely ever left it or had people to stay. There were never any children in this house."

"Mum – "

"*Do*," said the woman to Fran. "Do go and look around the garden. Perfectly safe. Far from the road."

The four adults walked away down the stone passage. A door to the dining-room was opened. "This," said the woman, "Is said to be the most beautiful dining-room in Kent."

"What was that?" asked Fran's mother. "Where is Fran?"

But Fran seemed happy. All four watched her in her white tee-shirt running across the grass. They watched her through the dining-room window all decorated round with frills and garlands of wisteria. "What a sweet girl," said the woman. The man cleared his throat and went wandering away.

"I think it's because there have never been any children in this house that it's in such beautiful condition," said the woman. "Nobody has even been unkind to it."

"I wouldn't say," said Fran's mother, "that children were – "

47

"Oh, but you can tell a house where children have taken charge. Now your dear little girl would never – "

The parents were taken into a room that smelled of rose-petals. A cherry-wood fire was burning although the day was very hot. Most of the fire was soft white ash. Somebody had been doing some needlework. Dogs slept quietly on a rug. "Oh, Fran would love – " said Fran's mother looking out of the window again. But Fran was not to be seen.

"Big family?" asked the old man suddenly.

"No. Just – Just one daughter, Fran."

"Big house for just one child."

"But you said there had never been children in this house."

"Oh – wouldn't say never. Wouldn't say never."

Fran had wandered away towards the garden but then had come in again to the stone hall, where she stopped to look at herself in a long dim glass. There was a blue jar with a lid on a low table, and she lifted the lid and saw a heap of dried rose-petals. The lid dropped back rather hard and wobbled on the jar as if to fall off. "Children are unkind to houses,"; she heard the floating voice of the woman shepherding her parents from one room to another. Fran pulled an unkind face at the jar. She turned a corner of the hall and saw the staircase sweeping upwards and round a corner. On the landing someone seemed to be standing, but then as she looked seemed not to be there after all. "Oh yes," she heard the woman's voice, "Oh yes, I suppose so. Lovely for children. The old nurseries should be very adequate. We never go up there."

"If there are nurseries," said Fran's father, "there must once have been children."

"I suppose so. Once. It's not a thing we ever think about."

"But if it has always been in your family it must have been inherited by children?"

"Oh cousins. Generally cousins inherited. Quite strange

how children have not been actually born here." Fran, who was sitting outside on the steps now in front of the open door, heard the little group clatter off along the stone pavement to the kitchens and thought, "Why are they going on about children so?"

She thought, "When they come back I'll go with them. I'll ask to see that painted man down the passage. I'd rather be with Mum to see him close."

Silence had fallen. The house behind her was still, the garden in front of her stiller. It was the moment in an English early-summer afternoon when there is a pause for sleep. Even the birds stop singing. Tired by their almost non-stop territorial squawks and cheeps and trills since dawn, they declare a truce and sit still upon branches, stand with heads cocked listening, scamper now and then in the bushes across dead leaves. When Fran listened very hard she thought she could just hear the swish of the road, or perhaps the sea. The smell of the early roses was very strong. Somewhere upstairs a window was opened and a light voice came and went as people moved from room to room. "Must have gone up the back stairs," Fran thought and leaned her head against the fluted column of the portico. It was strange. She felt she knew what the house looked like upstairs. Had she been upstairs yet or was she still thinking of going? Going. Going to sleep. Silly.

She jumped up and said, "You can't catch me. Bang, bang – you're dead."

She didn't know what she meant by it so she said it again out loud. "Bang, bang. You're dead."

She looked at the garden, all the way round from her left to her right. Nothing stirred. Not from the point where a high wall stood with a flint arch in it, not on the circular terrace with the round pond, not in the circle of green with the round gap in it where the courtyard opened to the long drive, and where their car was standing. The car made her feel safe.

Slowly round went her look, right across to where the stone

49

urns on the right showed a mossy path behind them. Along the path, out of the shadow of the house, the sun was blazing and you could see bright flowers.

Fran walked to the other side of the round pond and looked up at the house from the courtyard and saw the portrait again looking at her. It must be hanging in a very narrow passage, she thought, to be so near to the glass. The man was in some sort of uniform. You could see gold on his shoulders and lace on his cuffs. You could see long curls falling over his shoulders. Fancy soldiers with long curls hanging over their uniform! Think of the dandruff.

"Olden days," said Fran, "Bang, bang, you're dead," and she set off at a run between the stone urns and into the flower garden. "I'll run right round the house," she thought. "I'll run like mad. Then I'll say I've been all round the garden by myself, and not seen the ghost."

She ran like the wind all round, leaping the flower-beds, tearing along a showering rose-border, here and there, up and down, flying through another door in a stone wall among greenhouses and sheds and old stables, out again past a rose-red dove-house with the doves like fat pearls set in some of the little holes, and others stepping about the grass. Non-stop, non-stop she ran, across the lawn, right turn through a yew hedge, through the flint arch at last and back to the courtyard. "Oh yes," she would say to her friends on their bikes. "I did. I've been there. I've been all round the garden by myself and I didn't see a living soul."

"A *living* soul."

"I didn't see any ghost. Never even thought of one."

"You're brave, Fran. I'd never be brave like that. Are your parents going to buy the house?"

"Don't suppose so. It's very boring. They've never had any children in it. Like an old-folks home. Not even haunted."

Picking a draggle of purple wisteria off the courtyard wall – and pulling rather a big trail of it down as she did so – Fran began to do the next brave thing: to *walk* round the house. Slowly. She pulled a few petals off the wisteria and gave a carefree sort of wave at the portrait in the window. In front of it, looking out of the window, stood a little girl.

Then she was gone.

For less than a flick of a second Fran went cold round the back of the neck. Then hot.

Then she realised she must be going loopy. The girl hadn't been in a pinafore and frilly dress and long loose hair. She'd been in a white tee-shirt like Fran's own. She had been Fran's own reflection for a moment in the glass of the portrait.

"Stupid. Loopy," said Fran, picking off petals and scattering them down the mossy path, then along the rosy flag-stones of the rose garden. Her heart was beating very hard. It was almost pleasant, the fright and then the relief coming so close together.

"Well, I thought I saw the ghost but it was only myself reflected in a window," she'd say to the friends in the road at home.

"Oh Fran, you are brave."

"How d'you know it was you? Did you see its face? Everyone wears tee-shirts."

"Oh, I expect it was me all right. They said there'd never been any children in the house."

"What a cruddy house. I'll bet it's not true. I'll bet there's a girl they're keeping in there somewhere. Behind those bars. I bet she's being imprisoned. I bet they're kidnappers."

"They wouldn't be showing people over the house and trying to sell it if they were kidnappers. Not while the kidnapping was actually going on, anyway. No, you can tell —" Fran was explaining away, pulling off the petals. "There wasn't anyone there but me." She looked up at the windows in the stable-block she was passing. They were partly covered with creeper, but one of them stood open and a girl in a tee-shirt was sitting in it, watching Fran.

This time she didn't vanish. Her shiny short hair and white

51

shirt shone out clear. Across her humped-up knees lay a comic. She was very much the present day.

"It's you again," she said.

She was so ordinary that Fran's heart did not begin to thump at all. She thought, "It must be the gardener's daughter. They must live over the stables and she's just been in the house. I'll bet she wasn't meant to. That's why she ducked away."

"I saw you in the house," Fran said. "I thought you were a reflection of me."

"Reflection?"

"In the picture."

The girl looked disdainful. "When you've been in the house as long as I have," she said, "let's hope you'll know a bit more. Oil paintings don't give off reflections. They're not covered in glass."

"We won't be keeping the oil paintings," said Fran grandly. "I'm not interested in things like that."

"I wasn't at first," said the girl. "D'you want to come up? You can climb over the creeper if you like. It's cool up here."

"No thanks. We'll have to go soon. They'll wonder where I am when they see I'm not waiting by the car."

"Car?" said the girl. "Did you come in a car?"

"Of course we came in a car." She felt furious suddenly. The girl was looking at her oddly, maybe as if she wasn't rich enough to have a car. Just because she lived at The Elms. And she was only the gardener's daughter anyway. Who did she think she was?

"Well take care on the turn-out to the road then. It's a dangerous curve. It's much too hot to go driving today."

"I'm not hot," said Fran.

"You ought to be," said the girl in the tee-shirt, "with all that hair and those awful black stockings."

THREADS

I GOT a great-grandad going on ninety. He lives next door to us with my gran who's his daughter because she won't hear of Homes. Old folks going into them. She says it's something we could take notice of from the Japanese. They think it's the dregs, putting old folks away. And that's remarkable from my gran because she had a son in the war in Japanese hands and she never saw him more.

We live in Grangetown. Four generations in one street. It's not usual these days though not unheard of in Grangetown.

My great-grandad's no golden oldie, mind. My dad says he's a dreadful old man. Keeps his daughter running after him all day and half the night. "Where's me pills!" "Fetch me walking aid." "See to me foot." "Change me bed."

I never liked him. Not even when I was young. He just sits scowling, moving his foot up and down on the stirrup of the caliper. Squeaking. He makes this sort of grunt all the time. My dad says he's the only person he's ever met who snores when he's awake. He chews with his mouth and there's nothing in it. He never takes notice of me. Not ever. He never liked girls. He keeps on about having no grandsons, nor great-grandsons. His teeth keep dropping.

Well, I got stuck with him this Saturday afternoon. I like my gran and she wanted to go down the Middlesborough library where you can get a coffee. My mam was busy and my dad working – not that he'd have grandad-sat if he hadn't been working. Not him. They said, "Well, Karen can sit with him. For an hour. She's near fourteen. All she's to do is watch him for falls and run for his bottle if he needs it and empty it for him. It'll do her no harm."

I carried on at them. Once I wouldn't of. I was OK with

people once. I'd have said all right once, nice as pie. I don't know what's come over me these days. I hate thirteen.

But I like my gran, like I said, and she hardly gets out. When the nurse comes to bath great-grandad she'll do a dash down the post office for his pension. And for her pension. And maybe look in a couple of shop windows after the fashions. And that's all she gets. She's nearly seventy but she loves fashions. She likes her hair right, too, but it has to be shampoo and set only – there's no time for perms. She has to be thinking of him all the time – washing and ironing and cooking mushy food because of his gums. Collecting his pills from the surgery. Getting his lagers in. And not anything much in the way of thank-yous.

While she's out he'll walk up and down, up and down the passage on his walking frame and if he can he'll fall over to give her the frights when she comes running back in. My mam says, "He's a tyrant. She'll go first. Remember I've said it. She'll go first."

Well, this Saturday I didn't mind in the end sitting there with great-grandad because I'd got my period and I was feeling terrible. All I wanted was to sit still with a hot-water bottle and watch the football and not speak. When they'd gone, Mam and Gran, I humped myself down by the imitation coals on a stool, and folded my arms on my stomach and rocked myself about. He just sat there, in his special chair – it's like a throne – with his arms arranged over his walking frame and grunted away, paying me no attention.

They'd given him that telly gadget. A thing you hold in your hand and press. Well, you hardly have to press. You can just about breathe on the switch. When you do the television changes programme. It's like magic. Like an invisible thread. One minute you're seeing them tearing up and down all mud and curls kissing each other and everyone going mad in the stadium above the advertisements for brandy; then you're in a kitchen with sunshine and copper pans and a mother all apple blossom and aprons like you never see, pouring cocoa into mugs for a male model and a couple of soppy kids in a garden like seed-packets. Then whoops on the invisible thread and we're in black and white nostalgia valley and girls with patent leather lipstick and eyes like meat plates gazing at men in trilby hats and cigarettes at angles and someone's playing violins out of sight.

My great-grandad was still over the moon at this present. Over the moon. He even sometimes stopped snoring. "Ha," he kept saying, "Saves the carpet." "Ha – what's this next trash then?" "Ha – it's a goal. Looks as though the bugger's worth his transfer after all." He'd only had the thing a week.

I didn't have to do anything. Not even answer him. Just sit there and at four o'clock get him his cup of tea. So I sat and got warm over the electric bars and held on to my stomach and sucked a hanky end.

All of a sudden I noticed there was a silence and I opened my eyes. I'd fallen asleep with my head against the side of the mantelpiece and I'd jerked up. "Are you all right then?" I asked. I see he's looking over at me. Munching.

"Aye, I'm all right," he says. "Are you all right? Who are you?"

"Well, I'm Karen."

"Oh aye. I get you mixed. Are you Brian's?"

"Uncle Brian's dead," says I, "in Singapore. Long since."

"Oh aye," he says and sits and broods at the empty oblong of the telly.

I say, "You switched it off."

"Aye," he says. "There's not owt. Nowt that's anything."

"Don't you want the football?"

"They're all rubbish. Not a player among them."

"Did you play football once?"

"No. Never. Never played anything. Work – that's what I did."

He munched his lips and squeaked his caliper.

"D'you want your tea?" asks I and he looks across at me and says, "You looked twined."

55

"Twined?"

"Aye. Are you taken poorly?"

"No. I'll get you a cup of tea. I've got a pain, that's all."

"It'll be your time of the month," he said and I just looked.
Honest – I just looked.

It was right disgusting. I thought, you right disgusting old man.

I'll tell you something. I'll talk to my mam about most things – about drugs at school and sleeping with lads, and the pill, and whether people ought to live together before they're married like some I could mention in this family. (And it's not that I think it's wicked. Just disgusting and not romantic. It takes the poetry out and it's made our Marion a different person – all strong views and shouting. Brazen, if you want to know. And you should just see *him*!) Yes. I talk about a lot of things even to my dad and I talk to my gran about real things like death and why we are born and the stars and what started them, and religions.

But I won't talk about periods. No, I will not. Not even at school on games days. There's some can and some can't. You're born like it. Actually it has taken quite a bit of doing to write the word down. The whole thing's disgusting anyway. There was this girl in the church choir the only time I ever went. First question she asked. She was fourteen and I was ten. Disgusting.

And here's my great-grandad near on ninety talking about it matter-of-fact like he was a doctor or something. Which he never was. He was a farmer's son and then a leather merchant in Clitheroe.

And he scarcely knows who I am minute to minute. Yet he can speak it outright.

"It's from the moon," he says. "Women is in the hands of the moon. Like the tides. The time of the month. We're all on threads of one sort and another. It's best to be in charge of them, that's the secret. Hold 'em tight or snip 'em through." He breathed on the switch and the invisible thread tweaked the screen into life.

Well, before I *died*, I went out to the kitchen and boiled the kettle.

"Here's your tea then, great-grandad," I said. He was gazing at the television but the screen had gone blank again and the switch he'd let fall to the floor. "Put the cup down," he says. "Pull my table over. Look sharp now. Did you sugar it?" And he sat there slurping the tea through his loose teeth from the awful baby cup thing with the two handles.

"The moon," he says next, "I'll tell you something about the moon. And nowt to do with women and girls."

Squeak, squeak, squeak went the shoe on the caliper stirrup until I could have squealed. I tried to joke a bit. "Armour must have sounded like you," I said, but he just chewed his cheeks. He's no sense of humour.

"The moon," he says. "Nineteen-eight. We had a lad living with us on our farm at home. Irish boy. Couldn't read nor write. Skin and bone. They used to come over to Cumberland looking for work. Stood about all over the North-West at the hirings."

"Hirings?"

"Well, *hirings*. You – that's to say the farmers – would all go down the nearest market town a couple of times a year and walk about the square and there'd be little clusters of them – maybe a hundred. There'd be a wall and chalked up on it 'For Hire'. Not only Irish – Scotch fellers and Yorkshire and far afield. Lasses too. Standing about for hire and you'd take the strongest-looking."

"What, *people*?" says I. "Buying *people*?"

"No. Hiring. Aye. Nineteen-seven. Nineteen-eight. You'd take them home with you agreeing for a twelve-month or six months or just a haytime. The ones not chosen on account of being weak-looking stood around proud. They'd doss down in a hedgeback the night and then walk on to the next place.

"Well, there was this lad once – Michael – a poor thing, and

57

the boss, my father, was a kind man especially when he'd had a drink, which everyone had, hiring days, and he more than the rest. He'd been that long in the Public this day, to tell truth, most of the strong lads had been snapped up before he ever saw them. I hung about waiting and at last Father comes rolling along with his wing-collar under one ear and his green bowler hat on the back of his head – farmers dressed up them days for occasions. Here's this poor weak-headed little thing still standing there all alone with his mouth half open and his long Irish arms dangling out of his sleeves. 'Come on then, lad,' says the boss. 'Six months at five pounds, paid at finish, and here's your luck penny.' You had to give luck penny – which was a shilling – for right feelings, at hirings. That's all you did. No insurance. Nothing written. You learned them plenty, mind. It was being apprenticed. Six months and his keep. Their box would come on after on the train and they never had money for it. We'd pay the guard – meet it up at the nearest station after maybe a week and fetch it home on the cart.

"Well, this lad Michael was eighteen and I was eleven and he was like a brother to me. Work! He could work. Never to be called twice of a winter's morning. Five o'clock up for the cows and half of them milked before the boss even got to the byre. A fair demon he was for stacking the corn. He could fork a stack faster and straighter than the best – once he'd put weight on with a bit of proper cooking. You should have seen him eat. Plate a foot high. And he'd go down into it rather than take the food up into him. He didn't drink. Which was a queer carry-on for an Irishman. He said his mam had never let him. One thing he could do was shoot. He had this old gun. It'd been his father's. It was about all he owned. He and I'd be away off shooting many a summer night over the rough ground. Rooks for a pie. Cushets. Duck. He had a straight eye.

"Never a straight head though. There was a weakness there. He wasn't a thinker in any way. And not much will to

58

him. 'Simple,' my mother used to say. 'Poor Michael. He's a floddum. Well nigh a halfwit.' My father says, 'Nay. He'll do. There's nowt amiss with Michael except when the moon's full. He's not got what it takes to stand up against the moon,' and we'd all laugh. There's supposed to be something funny about folks going daft at time of full moon. Though it never seemed funny to me. Even before Michael.

"When the moon was full, see, Michael wouldn't work. He couldn't work. It seemed as if he just couldn't. He'd lie up in the barn and never rise off his bed. Now it sounds a terrible thing that he had to sleep in the barn but it weren't out of common. There was two – three cubicles up there with a bed and a chair and a box in each and a hook for clothes. We'd had three men once but times was harder now and we couldn't afford but one. He'd come down and wash at the yard pump, and his needs he'd do behind the hedges. He ate his food with us – across at another table in the kitchen, but in the same room. We weren't savages. We'd try teaching him whist and nap of an evening too, but he couldn't get his mind round the numbers on the cards.

"When the moon was full though, Michael was nowhere in the kitchen. He never came in for his food and he never came down to the pump to wash. Nor put on his clothes. No more did he go off after the cows for milking, nor pick up the chain to take the bull to the water, nor down to the stack-yard, nor away shooting cushets with me. The gun stood propped against the wall of his barn-stall, and the boss would roar and create, but Michael would just lie there with his eyes wide open, not speaking, humped on his iron bed under his blanket and old raggedy coat, watching the ivy at the barn slats flickering. 'Leave him be,' the boss'd say at finish. 'It's the moon. He's one of them poor devils affected. He's beyond us all. Three days and he'll be back.'

"My mother would take food up there to Michael against the boss's orders but he never touched it. She'd set it on the chair beside him, talking kind and natural.

"Then a day or so after, he'd be down at the pump again, smiling round, washing himself and the plates Mother had brought. Whistling. He'd cleared the plates all at once with his fingers to such a polish they scarcely needed water.

"Well, he left.

"We had to put him off after next harvest. Times was bad. I walked with him to the lonning gate and said goodbye and he went off to the next hiring. He had a better coat than when he came for we'd given him the boss's old one. There was a good shirt in his bundle and some butter and a bit of bacon and five shillings over his five pounds. He looked a better buy than six months previous, his gun across his shoulder almost jaunty. He loved that gun.

"Well next thing we know he's up for murder.

"Michael up for murder. 'The gentlest lad we ever had,' my father says. 'Never had a drink in him. Never a word of bad language.'

"It seems the next farmer to hire him had been a brute, however. Yelled at him and cussed at him morning to night and put him out of the house after supper like a dog. When Michael came to his funny turn at the time of the full moon he'd pulled him from his bed and kicked him. The second day he did it again and Michael upped from the floor – quiet, sweet-charactered Michael – and took the gun and shot the farmer through the head.

"My father, the boss, put on his wing-collar and his bowler hat and his button boots and his best suit and went to speak for Michael at the trial. Miles away. Over in the North-East. Further than my father had even been in his life. But it did no good. He told them about the full moon. But it did not a bit of good. They hanged Michael. In Durham gaol. Nineteen-eight. He was just nineteen."

"*Now* then!" In comes my gran all pink in the face in what looks very like a new scarf, and carrying parcels and two library books and followed by my mam with the supermarket shopping and a big plotted plant.

"Are you right then?" says Mam. "How's he been? You saw to his tea? My, I could do with some. Mother's brought you a plant, Grandad – begonia, the kind you like. Only a pound. Whatever's the matter with the telly? It's not on."

"Are you better?" asks my gran. "Sit still and I'll get the tea."

"I'm fine," says I. "Great. I'll get it. I'll get it for all of us. There's nothing wrong with me at all."

"That's a good lass," says Gran, and follows me to the kitchen. "Has he been difficult? He's looking very wambly. It'd be dull for you – all alone on a Saturday afternoon. Your poor grandad, there's not much there any more I'm afraid. We'll all come to it. He's got interest and memory for nothing now, poor soul."

RODE BY ALL WITH PRIDE

Marjorie Partridge at the end of her garden savaged the earth around the hydrangeas and wept for her child, Olivia.

Wimbledon gardens can be venerable. Even Tudor. Marjorie's garden was only nineteenth-century but it had had a hundred years of care, seventy-five of them from a chain of full-time gardeners, now forgotten.

Wimbledon is not the suburb of the plastic greenhouse, tomato plant, sunflower and prize marrow; the squirl of coloured glass in the vestibule window, permanent-wave and coffee morning, of wife-swopping and vodka. This is folklore. It is – or the enclave of red roads round the Common is – one cannot speak for down the hill – a serious, rich and confident place which does not follow fashion.

The enclave is the old town and as in the old town in Rabat or Delhi or Paris or Dublin it breathes its own air. Like many old towns there is still money there – the best sort of money: old, invisible, slow-burning, undiscussed and never used in idiot beautification. Marjorie had not had a new coat in years. Her shoes were funny. Her drawing-room curtains were very old and her Turkey rugs, though nearly priceless, were worn and frayed down to the knots. In Hampstead a house with a Picasso in its safe has grilles to its windows when the owners are away. In Old Wimbledon, when there is a Braque on the wall (the Partridges had a Kandinsky) there is only the most antique of burglar alarms hidden in the creeper. There is however a Veronica or a Phyllis or a Mrs Something who moves in until the holiday is over to keep things looking occupied. These people cost more than grilles in the end and are not so smart, but they are more effective. They are also interesting, being the last trickle of the Edwardian servant class which staffed and enlivened these twenty or so streets until the Wars. The Partridges' house – and it was not ostentatious – had five indoor servants until 1939, Marjorie had been told, not to mention gardeners. Now, as she was fond of saying, "There is only me – and Maureen. And of course Mr Jackson who sees to things outside."

Maureen and Mr Jackson were not only better dressed than the Partridges. They had more comfortable and warmer houses, more ready cash, more holidays, more laughs, more sex, more entertaining lives. But there existed between them and their employers a queer mutual confidence, a feudal equality and a genuine loyalty that was very like love. They had stayed – Maureen and Mr Jackson – for years.

Thus Mr Jackson would crash into Mrs Partridge's conservatory when she was reading Solzhenitsyn and roar, "Your boiler's done for. It's new central heating now. Can't complain. Old in the sixties – and before that. We're none of us what we were." Maureen the cleaner – who called herself housekeeper on the telephone but was otherwise without vice – knew Majorie's most inward thoughts, could say anything to her. "You look better the less you try," she would observe through the bedroom door as Marjorie gazed sternly at herself in some old fur; and, "You and I understand each other, Mrs Partridge." She had known Mrs Partridge's daughter Olivia since the shawl, and although Maureen's days were Mondays, Wednesdays and Fridays (mornings) and Olivia killed herself on a Tuesday afternoon it was Maureen who was first at the house. She lived in Morden – a good three-quarters of an hour.

Mr Partridge had left the previous morning for Thailand via the Middle East and Dacca, and was just about arriving in Bangkok as Maureen reached Rathbone Road. He was a civil servant in high office, a tiny, yellow-faced, pre-aged man, not clubbable. He seldom spoke at the few Christmas drinks parties he attended in the enclave but was very welcome at them and would have been very sorry not to have been asked.

He was known as "old Jack Partridge – bloody clever". He read a great deal – Descartes – in the French of course – Hobbes, Keynes; but Thomas Hardy too, and Brecht, and Becket. At the cinema – the Partridges did not watch television and did not have a set – he very much enjoyed Woody Allen. Unstuffy Jack Partridge, immensely able, up to date, seeing both *Private Eye* and *The Times Literary Supplement*.

And no one could say that he had ever expected too much of Olivia. He had never pushed her in any way. There had been been no need. Dreamy and cool, Olivia had always seemed to live without stress. Yes, Jack Partridge knew that he had the measure of nearly all his colleagues at work. Yes, he had got a First at Cambridge and later at Harvard. Yes, he could run rings round his Minister and such members of the Cabinet as dared present themselves before him; and when he dined on high table at his old college, such Fellows as were forewarned sharpened themselves up in advance. Yes, he knew that only Marjorie who had also taken a First – in English at Oxford – very much the woman's subject in those days, but still – yes, he knew that only Marjorie could stand up to him in rational day to day logic; and yes, he knew that the pair of them must be rather formidable parents for an only child.

But not for Livie.

Jack Partridge had loved his daughter from the day he first met her in St Teresa's Maternity Hospital along the Ridgway. In those days it was run by crackling long-skirted nuns, and quite cheap, not as later the resting place for millionaires, often foreigners. It was the unquestioned lying-in place for the memsahibs of the enclave and many of them had met there and long friendships had begun. In the private room at St Teresa's Jack had noted for the first time his daughter's silky hair, her bland reflective sleeping face, had moved a sensitive finger, later that evening to turn the pages of official reports, along her cheek. "Olivia," he had said.

"'Olivia Partridge'," had said Marjorie, looking down at

the cot. Marjorie was rosy and large – an awfully nice woman –
huge-bosomed on the high bed, for she was of course going to
breast-feed. A Double First was by the way in the sixties.
Educated women were fulfilled by their memories and moved
on with intensity and dedication to bring up their children
themselves. They read the FT with the baby on their
shoulder, kept up *The Times* crossword and at least one
foreign language. They baked cakes, wrote letters to each
other and when the children were old enough to be at school
all day had pleasant times at Hatchards and the University
Women's Club for lunch. Feminism's self-awareness, self-
love, was in Wimbledon strictly for the future – though less
than ten miles away in Richmond it was already knocking on
the Georgian doors, seeping through the wisterias and round
the glossy dining tables. Richmond women were rushing
upstairs weeping and packing suitcases, or asking young men
to lunch and to stay the afternoon. But a curious class of
person has always lived in Richmond.

"'Olivia Partridge'," said her mother, eighteen years ago
at St Teresa's in her sensible long-sleeved nightdress, surrounded by the garden flowers of local friends and a photograph of Jack doing his army service in the Education Corps,
"'Olivia Partridge' – oh dear, it does sound rather like a don."

"She's beautiful," said old Jack and put her in the paper,
which is to say *The Times*: "To Jack and Marjorie Partridge, a
daughter, Olivia," and entered her name for Sherborne
School and took out another couple of insurance policies. The
satisfaction he felt about Olivia became the deep part of his
life. He was unconcerned that no other child followed her.
Neither parent was young.

Olivia went first to Mrs Parsons's nice little school on the
Common which didn't fuss about examinations like the High
School. The little girls spent a great deal of time doing
Nature, with Miss Phillips puffing behind them up to Caesar's
Camp. Twice a week they played Rounders under the twisted
chestnut tree opposite South Side, which had given shelter to

generations of Wimbledon nannies even before Robert Graves was patted under it in his pram by Swinburne. It was gentle Rounders, and consisted largely in Miss Phillips's calling out encouragement and shaking tidy the heap of brown cardigans that were used as base; and in the making of daisy chains. Marjorie, striding by on a walk with the dog, used to pretend not to see Livie, thoughtfully fielding, for she knew that a child must develop its private life at school.

Which – the Partridges never put a foot wrong, ever – Livie did. She was clearly very clever, and so self-reliant that at seven she was making two or three trips a week to the Public Library down the hill.

The parent Partridges, living in Rathbone Road, had no need of down-the-hill themselves. Jack was a member of the London Library which took care of books. Friends, shops, restaurants, fresh air, exercise, Church (Livie was not deprived of the chance of Christianity though her parents were not believers and they explained this to her) were all available within the enclave. Jack did not even have to walk down the hill to the station but took a bus to Putney and then the tube. Chauffeurs were for foreigners and the media people on Drax Avenue and Parkside.

But Olivia devoured books so fast that the down-the-hill library was vital to her and she was found sitting – aged eight – in the Reference Room in Compton Road among all the hackers and spitters and tramps clinking bottles and old creatures taking grey sandwiches out of paper bags, and looking very happy. It shocked her mother who rousted her out. "My *dear*!" she said to her friends. "She was oblivious. You know, she is off this earth!"

"Oblivious Olivious," said Jack. "Oblivia Olivia!" It became quite a joke.

Marjorie did occasionally go down the hill to meet Jack in the car off the Waterloo train when he was late and this was a quicker way home. She hated it – sitting in the station forecourt, a place nobody has ever loved (waiting-time

mercifully restricted to ten minutes) watching the army of
pale men emerge from the underground like souls from hell.
Over the years she saw known faces growing greyer, lines
between nose and mouth cut deeper, good suits become more
expensive, less noticeable, briefcases more importantly battered. Some talked to themselves, head down, turning for the
hill to walk, for health's sake, home. "So alike," thought
Marjorie. "Some day I'll drive off the wrong one."

"Jack," she said. "I'm finished with down-the-hill. When
you come home by train you'll have to get a taxi."

"Why?"

"Oh they are such awful people down there. Or else just
those poor tired men."

"The country's run by us. The poor, tired men," he said.
"You ought to thank God for us. We watch over govern-
ments, the tired men. And I suppose women. A few. We're
the protectors. Didn't Cromwell live at The Crooked Billet?"

"Nonsense. Cromwell was Huntingdon."

"It's said."

"I expect it was Thomas. He probably once walked over
the Common. You only have to have a cup of tea in
Wimbledon for them to put up a blue plaque to you."

"There isn't a blue plaque for a Cromwell."

"I don't suppose dear old Wimbledon ever heard of either
Cromwell while he was alive. It's always been pretty
private."

The Crooked Billet is the pretty, countrified pub near the
green end of Rathbone Road. It faces a famous seventeenth
century house – famous of course only within the enclave:
protected from general acclaim – which never has its windows
washed and where there are said to be Rembrandts. It is
alongside the site of a mansion pulled down the year Livie was
born where Pitt the Younger used to spend his country
weekends. Pitt the Younger, like Jack Partridge and the hosts
of the grey-faced men on the underground, is on record as
saying that he would have cracked without the blessedness of

Wimbledon Common at weekends. It stretched gently then, unchangingly, to Roehampton, smelling of hay and flowers as it does still. "Thank God for the Common," Jack would say, whistling up the dog. "Coming Livie?" and they would walk to the windmill and down into the woods. "It sparkles," said Livie on a windy, watery day. "Like a Corot," said her father, and Livie nodded. At eight she knew what a Corot was.

The woods had a pool in them called Queensmere where Wimbledon gentlemen (Jack had not met any of them) were allowed to bathe naked before eight o'clock in the morning. It was all very respectable and sylvan, and the three Partridges laughed about it sometimes for fun. But Livie, writing of it in an essay for Miss Phillips, "The Place Where I Live", had this part crossed out in broad, green ink.

Queensmere after that, a murky place, was bewildering to her. She couldn't like it anyway because quite soon after the essay her father had told her that someone – some "poor, uncertain lady" – had drowned herself there long ago. "It was winter. They found her in the morning and her hair was spread out in spikes, frozen in the ice. Unpleasant business." Jack was a Wimbledonian – born in the enclave. He knew the legends.

"I never told you that," he said years later. "It was your mother I told. 'Uncertain lady' – really Olivia! As if I'd say that to a child."

But he often tended to get his two women mixed up.

On June the fifth every year a Fair comes to Wimbledon Common and you can hear its thump and beat as far away as Putney Hill. First come the big caravans, shuttered and huge. They arrive by night, as they have done perhaps since Pitt the Younger. One morning they are found resting there like birds from Africa. For two days they sleep, then spring to life the third evening, blazing and blaring and whirling with lights like musical fireworks. The ring of houses of the enclave sits darkly by, for the Fair people have nothing to do with the people of the enclave (their evening customers come from Tooting, even Streatham) and the enclave pretends that the Fair is not there, even when the lights play over their faces as they lie in bed. For two weeks the flickers and strains of the Zharooms and the Bumpums and the Tunnel of Love and the wonderful Golden Horses ("Rode by all with Pride") take charge of the Common's central platform near the War Memorial as they did the day Marjorie brought Olivia home in her arms from the hospital run by the excellent nuns. For years Olivia thought that the Fair was some demonstration in honour of her birthday and had been so old when she had realised that this was not so (maybe ten – even eleven) that she blushed to think of it.

At eleven Olivia did not go away to Sherborne School after all as she won a magnificently important scholarship to a famous London day school. The decision to accept it had been entirely hers, said the Partridges, and she was doing special subjects there – Greek, Russian – in no time at all. "It seems young," they said. "But the school think she's up to it. We don't interfere." She was keeping up her Music too – begun at Mrs Parsons's – and attending the Royal College in Marylebone on Saturday mornings. On Sundays for nearly a year, she took Confirmation classes, and then did voluntary work through the local church – there was an old lady she went to see in Bathgate Road and a spastic boy in The Drive. "My dear, we never *see* her," her mother said to friends at lunches. Jack, dining in Geneva or Berlin, said, "Yes. One girl. No – London day school. More in touch we think. Doing Russian – and it's to be Chinese next I hear. Yes – very young. Well – Cambridge, we rather hope."

But he never boasted, was never excessive, never mentioned Olivia without being asked. Marjorie, digging her brussels sprouts or writing a little monograph on *George Eliot at Southfields* for the Wimbledon Lit. and Sci. (Literary and Scientific Society, founded 1891) was sensible likewise. She would smile down at her spade or out of the study window at the gate, watching Olivia coming home (she looks tired, thought Marjorie, but you do look tired in your O level year) – Marjorie would smile and indulge in quick fantasies that it would be Oxford Olivia plumped for – that her first term, leaves falling, green lawns, sloping to the river – she would settle Olivia in at her own old college. Perhaps into her own old room.

Livie didn't do particularly well in the O Levels, though the school said that this hardly mattered. O Levels are no test of a mind. Marjorie and the Headmistress had quite a smile about how much better some of Livie's contemporaries had done with not a tenth of Livie's brilliance. Livie proceeded to Russian, Greek and Mathematics at Advanced Level. She continued her Music. Her piano playing was now astonishing. "I wouldn't say exactly *concert* standard," said Marjorie, laughing as if she were lying a little. Livie took on secretary-ships of many societies and became Head Girl. She organised dances to which boys were invited, though she did not meet any of them socially – or dance. She stood gravely by the disco looking beautiful but in heavy, low-heeled shoes.

She looked tireder – but no wonder. Marjorie took to making lightning dashes to the school to fetch her home – sometimes finding that there was a long wait when she got there. But she had the car radio and a heater and her petit-point. Often she found that she and Livie had missed each other and Livie was at home before her – head back, eyes shut on the porch seat having forgotten her keys. Livie was vague now about her time-table, vague even about where she had been. Marjorie gave up the petit-point at the school gate. Livie had never been enthusiastic about her mother coming to fetch her anyway. Not even at Mrs Parsons's.

"Is she overdoing things?" Marjorie wanted to ask the Headmistress. But Livie was seventeen. The Headmistress was statuesque and looked as if she had never needed a mother. Anyhow, Marjorie hated women who fussed to

Headmistresses.

The Fair arrived during the Advanced Levels. It was louder than ever this year with some new and wilder variety of music. Marjorie – Jack was away – almost thought of moving up into London, near to the school during the examinations – perhaps to a private hotel – but Livie looked amazed. She was used to the Fair's arrival during examination days. The noise was familiar to her, washed beautifully over her. It had never interfered with sleep or work. And it was part of her birthday. She opened her bedroom windows wide and the night before the Greek Unseen paper Marjorie went up with milk and glucose to find Livie's curtains flapping, books put tidily away and Livie not there. It was past ten o'clock. Livie came in after midnight.

"Livie! where were you?"

"I went round the Fair."

"Alone?"

"Yes, Pride of the South. 'Rode by all with Pride.' It says it in scrolls."

"Have you been in The Crooked Billet? Are you drunk?"

"I've been to the Fair. The Golden Horses aren't there. They've been smashed up. He said it would be too expensive to repair them. 'Rode by all with pride.' "

"Are you well? Are you all right?"

"They were Italian," said Livie. "Very old. Lovely wrong grammar. All gone. It was vandals."

But she seemed herself in the morning.

She did all right in the A Levels. All right. Nothing spectacular. There were some spectacular results that year and some girls were even given university places uncondition- ally. One of these girls was also found to be pregnant, not in favour of abortion and desirous of keeping the baby. Her mother – a Kensington woman – had a nervous breakdown and took herself off to the South of France, so that one unconditional university place was going to be wasted. "There are people with *real* problems," wrote Marjorie to

Jack in Tokyo, and Jack went straight out and bought Livie some pearl stud earrings (Minimoto, like her mother's) and wrote her a delightful letter saying how little he worried about her. She was splendid. She had to remember that she was a really splendid person. "For Oxford," he said (it *was* to be Oxford), "It is the entrance examination and the personal interview that counts. I confidently predict – and remember, Livie, I am not unastute at prediction though I dare say it is a thing I would only admit to you or your mother – I confidently predict that no tutor in his right mind could ever turn you down. You are very special." And he went on to talk about the economy of Japan.

He added a post-script. She was to remember the triviality of examinations. The hazards of being accepted by Oxbridge were to her trifling. The real assessments of her, the true tests of the brain were to come. Quality was after all – except for the bourgeois – only apparent after the first Degree, at post-graduate level. "So it won't all be over by Christmas, old girl. Don't think you're at the end yet."

The Partridges were parents in a million, loving, kind and good. They spoke eye-ball to eye-ball, man to man.

The Oxford entrance examination was still an autumn away and so Marjorie made a great point of seeing that Livie had some fun during the summer holidays. She arranged for her to go to some of the private dances in the enclave arranged by the Wives' Fellowship. These were by invitation only to big houses in Marryat and Bathgate Road and even one in a quaint house over towards Raynes Park belonging to a woman married to a Greek (an unfortunate result of reading Modern Languages at Hull) but who was third-generation Wimbledon and a super girl. One knows simply everyone at these dances, said Marjorie, that's what's so nice, and if some of them speak in common voices and wear one earring one knows that it is just showing off. They'll be sending their own children to Wives' Dances one day. You could tell just to look at them – pink hair, earrings and the lot. As Robert Graves said in *Goodbye to all That* – and Robert Graves of course was born just off the Ridgway, down the road from Livie – you can always tell a gentleman. These young people were gents. It would have been none of them for example who had smashed the stone lions which had stood for a hundred years outside the vet's in the High Street. Heaven alone knew who those people might be.

Livie was writing something slowly across the kitchen window as her mother's view of Robert Graves and the vet's lions was being put forward. She had just come home from one of the dances – she always came home alone. She turned eyes of such desolation on Marjorie that Marjorie stopped laying the breakfast.

"Livie?"

"The vet's lions," said Livie. "My God."

"Now Livie – "

"My God."

"Aren't you pleased that the people at the dance didn't smash the vet's lions?"

"My God."

"Livie! They've been repaired by the John Evelyn Society."

"Do you see John Evelyn on the vet's lions?"

"Now Livie – Well, no Livie. No Livie, of course I don't. They used to stand on some gateposts about then – Evelyn's time – I believe. Some great house. I don't think he actually lived in Wimbledon you know. Just passed through."

"A lot of them," said Livie. "Did that."

"The Thackerays would have known them of course. I expect Anne Thackeray must actually have sat on them. You all sat on them of course, *all* the children at Mrs Parsons's."

"Rode by all with pride."

"Livie – whatever's wrong? Just get out the marmalade, would you? Swinburne must have known them of course. He'd have passed them every day on the way to The Rose and Crown before getting his newspaper from Frost's. At the

74

second door. Did you know, Livie – Frost's had two doors. Until just last year when they pulled it down they called the second door 'Mr Swinburne's door'. Isn't it killing?"

"Killing."

"Livie – "

But Livie had walked away.

"Olivia's getting a bit cantankerous – just a little bit difficult," wrote Marjorie to Jack. "'It's natural I suppose. We have been so lucky – and looking round we still are so lucky. Sometimes you might almost think it was something to do with this place, the disasters there are on all sides. And yet I'm sure there's no place more caring. I suppose there is always disaster with the young. 'Youth is a blunder' – Disraeli. Did I tell you about Michael B. in Bicester Crescent? He's had something they call a breakdown (drugs?) and he's in The Priory. *Brilliant* A Levels. He's been sleeping rough on the Common." Later she wrote, "Those poor Smiths on Ridgway Hill. Ophelia has gone off to Tooting to live with an Iranian. She's been in trouble with the police. She met him in this so-called wine-bar. And do you remember little Duffy Duff? Apparently he left Cambridge without a Degree. Went in to each exam and just walked out again. He's so good they say they would have given him something if he had only written his name on the paper. All he wrote was 'not to be classified'. Oh, isn't it sad – do you remember him reciting that lovely little ballad at the end-of-term Christmas concert? He looked like a little angel himself. He's helping to run a Meditation Centre in the Lake District now and when he rang his father up the other day to wish him happy birthday – which is something I suppose: Mrs Parsons's training! - he was talking in broadest Cockney! I don't suppose anybody understands a word he says, especially in the Lake District. Oh how lucky we are with Livie."

Livie, the day of the Oxford entrance papers, had the composure and quietness of the day she was born. Her tall figure in good skirt and jersey, her hair well cut – she went to Marjorie's girl at Peter Jones – delighted some of her mother's friends who passed her on the way to the bus. "Dear Livie," they said. "Her smile hasn't changed since they were all at dancing class."

"I'd not say that," said Maureen, passing through the Partridge's hall – jumble was being sorted – "Keeps herself to herself. Always did. But I'll not say she's never changed. There's different bits to Olivia. I'll not forget when I used to take her to watch the Fair."

"Oh, she always liked the Fair."

"Made me go on that Ghost Train. Sick as a dog."

"Were you, Maureen?" Marjorie carefully avoided her friends' eyes in case someone laughed. Maureen was a card. "You shouldn't have given way to her."

"No – *I* weren't sick. She were. Olivia was the one sick. She didn't care though. She loved them rotors, too. Stuck to the side of the drum she was with her skirt above her head. And she got me to take her up on them golden horses too – them things with barley sugars skewered through them diagonal and their heads tossed back and their teeth glaring out. Both arms round their necks and her hair all streamed out like Godiva."

"Maureen is sometimes quite coarse," said Marjorie to Jack over carré of lamb from the butcher in the High Street who delivered, and put frills on the cutlets. Olivia was out – probably something to do with the spastic or the old lady – not church, which she had given up. She had been uncommunicative that morning and since the Oxford entrance papers. "Maureen said that Livie used to scream at the Fair with her skirt over her face."

"Not much harm in that. And very long ago if it was when Maureen used to take her. By the way, which day does she hear?"

"Oh quickly. The interview is this week. On Wednesday –

Oxford is quite quick."

"Oh Lord – then I shall be away?"

"Yes of course. Didn't you know?"

"At Cambridge I think they took longer to tell us. Or was it shorter?"

"I don't think you need worry about not being here. She's much less fussed than either of us. And we're only fussed because – well, not because she might not get in. That would be ridiculous. I suppose we're really just excited. It's an emotional time. It doesn't seem a minute since this was happening to me. After all – it's a very big moment, getting into Oxbridge."

"You know," said Jack, "I don't remember it. It was taken for granted. Just part of life then if you were any good at all. Less pressure then."

"Oh – Livie's had no pressure. Not from us. Good heavens, she knows, even if there were some lunacy and she didn't – well, as if we'd think any less of her!"

"Well of course. Marjorie – I suppose she *will* get an interview?"

"Well, of course she'll get an interview. It's only the absolute unknowns who don't. And heavens, I've always been very close to Mabel Pye. It'll cause a great deal of surprise if she doesn't, I must say – I've written round several people to say that she may be looking in on Wednesday afterwards for a cup of tea. Goodness, at school they say she's the best they've had in ten years. It's not the possibility of interviews they're all thinking about. It's the kind of Award she'll get. Just wait till we're all hearing that she's the first woman at All Souls."

"Now then Marjorie. This letter – the letter giving the time of the interview comes when?"

"It doesn't come. They all have to be at the college on Wednesday *unless* there is a letter. If a letter comes it's to say they're not wanted."

"A pretty devastating business. Rather cruel."

"It's fairly new, I think. Oh, I don't think we need worry about letters."

Jack trickled perfect mint-sauce over his lamb. "We should chop back the mint," he said. "It's tending to get above itself."

"I've done it. I've had the parsley out, too. Time to re-sow."

"It's time to divide the irises. And bring in the dahlias." He looked at his disciplined garden, programmed for Spring. It was getting near Christmas. Next door a neighbour, a fashionable lawyer, was giving one of his drinks parties. The women could be heard screaming in gusts as the front door opened and shut. "I'd rather my women screamed at the Fair than next door," said Jack. "Just listen to them – baying for gin. The road's changing."

"Oh – I don't know."

"Oxford we're going to find changed, too, you know. I warn you. I was talking – ."

"Oh well – of course we are. It must. To a certain extent. But there'll always be some like us. A nucleus – ."

"Feminism," said Jack. "Lesbianism. Free love or whatever they call it nowadays. This pill business."

"We needn't worry about Livie."

"Over-work – ."

"Livie's *never* over-worked. Her mind's not even been stretched yet. She's not a worrier. Livie's the most peaceful person I know."

They walked, Jack and Marjorie, on the Common that afternoon meeting several friends. Most of these also walked in pairs, for divorce and early death are remarkably rare in the enclave. Most were without children. Their children were grown and flown. The Partridges called out to them and they called back in similar pleasant old-fashioned voices. "Any news of Adrian?" "Is Francesca still at the BBC?" "I hear Camilla's in at Girton – not a bit surprised." "Good luck to Livie on Wednesday."

The calls were passwords, codes, the names of the measures of a dance. They meant more than they seemed to mean. They meant, "We are a tribe. A club. We think alike. We have done our best. We have brought up our children to follow us on, which is ancient and natural but nowadays courageous. We act for the common good."

The calls said that there had been many shared years – first with prams, then push-chairs, then small bikes, then ponies from the riding school: changeless Miss Thompson's dancing class, Guy Fawkes parties and Hallowe'ens; that there had been year after year of birthdays on the Common, the cake carried, with candles separate, to be assembled in the long grass with the flowers in it by The Causeway or The Pound or in the secret, woody parts round Queensmere. The calls said that all nice children have clean hair, that to Christmas tea parties they bring small presents, prettily wrapped, and the boys wear bow ties and the girls long white socks and pretty dresses, not jeans.

The words said, "We and our children belong to a time before the Beatles, before the recession, before we all drank wine every day although it was so cheap, to a time when you could buy cakes like you make at home in the High Street and none of us had heard of a video centre or seen a launderette; a time when you could drive down Church Road in tennis fortnight and even park there. And the tennis players were still gentlemen like Robert Graves. When at the Fair the Golden Horses flew."

The words said, "We are the elect. By many we suppose we are considered dreadful. We are all true blue, even if we are radicals, or the odd eccentric socialist. We are staunch, we are loyal, we are innocent in a way, bless us. We are rather happy people and when bad times come we comfort one another."

The enclave was out in force that afternoon, their dogs bounding round them. Such people and dogs not of the enclave who passed, passed like shadows. Marjorie, contented, thought, "This is my landscape," and uncharacteristically took Jack's hand, as the sun went down suddenly behind Queensmere in a scar of white light.

On Tuesday after the second post and the last nonsensical thought of a rejecting letter was past, Marjorie went down the hill to the station to buy Olivia's return ticket to Oxford for the next day. She had decided, rather wisely she thought, not to drive her there. "It is Livie's day," she said to herself on the hill, "Livie's life. I have always seen to that." She remembered all at once the long-ago Rounders game by the twisted chestnut tree on the corner of South Side, and Livie, reflective in the long grass; how she had turned away from the child, not wanting Livie to feel that she was watching to see whether or not she caught the ball. "And Livie knew," she thought. She stopped in surprise. "Livie knew – Livie has always known all about me. And Jack. She's never said anything. Never said that she – loved us, for instance. We never said these things to each other, any of us. We never said it to her even when she was a baby."

"She'll be touched, though, that I've been down to get the ticket," she thought. "When I get home I will put it into her hand."

But when Marjorie got home Livie was not about. The enclave was silent. Marjorie made herself tea and sat by the telephone to wait for Jack's call to say that he had safely reached Bangkok. Rathbone Road was still. Marjorie slept.

Later, two waited with her, Maureen in the kitchen in her coat, motionless, and Mr Jackson outside, standing like wood beside the bleached and undivided irises.

Marjorie at the end of the garden savaged the earth around the hydrangeas. She wept and dug, dug and wept.

SWAN

❧

Two boys walked over the bridge.

They were big boys from the private school on the rich side of the river. One afternoon each week they had to spend helping people. They helped old people with no one to love them and younger children who were finding school difficult. It was a rule.

"I find school difficult myself," said Jackson. "Exams for a start."

"I have plenty of people at home who think no one loves them," said Pratt. "Two grandparents, two parents, one sister."

"And all called Pratt, poor things," said Jackson, and he and Pratt began to fight in a friendly way, bumping up against each other until Jackson fell against a lady with a shopping-trolley on a stick and all her cornflakes fell out and a packet of flour, which burst.

"I'm going straight to your school," she said. "I know that uniform. It's supposed to be a good school. I'm going to lay a complaint," and she wagged her arms up and down at the elbows like a hen. Pratt, who often found words coming out of his mouth without warning, said, "Lay an egg. Cluck."

"That's done it. That's finished it," said the woman. "I'm going right round now. *And* I'll say you were slopping down the York Road Battersea at two o'clock in the afternoon, three miles from where you ought to be."

"We are doing our Social Work," said Pratt. "Helping people."

"Helping people!" said the woman, pointing at the pavement.

"We're being interviewed to take care of unfortunate

children," said Jackson.

"They're unfortunate all right if all they can get is you."
And she steamed off, leaving the flour spread about like
snow, and passers-by walked over it giving dark looks and
taking ghostly footprints away into the distance. Pratt eased
as much of it as he could into the gutter with his feet.

"She's right," he said. "I don't know much about
unfortunate children. Or any children."

"They may not let us when they see us," said Jackson.
"Come on. We'd better turn up. They can look at us and form
an opinion."

"Whatever's that mess on your shoes?" asked the Head
Teacher at the school on the rough side of the river, coming
towards them across the hall. "Dear me. It *is* a nasty day.
How do you do? Your children are ready for you, I think.
Maybe today you might like just to talk to them indoors and
start taking them out next week?"

"Yes, please," said Jackson.

"Taking them *out*?" said Pratt.

"Yes. The idea is that – with the parents' consent – you
take them out and widen their lives. Most of them on this side
of the river never go anywhere. It's a depressed area. Their
lives are simply school (or truanting), television, bed and
school, though we have children from every country in the
world."

"It's about the same for us," said Pratt. "Just cross out
television and insert homework."

"Oh, come now," said the Head Teacher, "you do lots of
things. Over the river, there's the Zoo and all the museums
and the Tower of London and all the lovely shops. All the
good things happen over the bridge. Most of our children
here have scarcely seen a blade of grass. Now – you are two
very reliable boys, I gather?" (She looked a bit doubtful.)
"Just wipe your feet and follow me."

She opened a door of a classroom, but there was silence

82

inside and only one small Chinese boy looking closely into the side of a fish-tank.

"Oh dear. Whatever … ? Oh, of course. They're all in the gym. This is Henry. Henry Wu. He doesn't do any team-games. Or – anything, really. He is one of the children you are to try to help. Now which of you would like Henry? He's nearly seven."

"I would," said Pratt, wondering again why words kept emerging from his mouth.

"Good. I'll leave you here then. Your friend and I will go and find the other child. Come here Henry and meet – what's your name?"

"Pratt."

"Pratt. HERE'S PRATT, HENRY. He's not deaf, Pratt. Or dumb. He's been tested. It is just that he won't speak or listen. He shuts himself away. PRATT, HENRY," she said, and vanished with an ushering arm behind Jackson, closing the door.

Henry Wu watched the fish.

"Hello," said Pratt after a while. "Fish."

He thought, that is a very silly remark. He made it again, "Fish."

The head of Henry Wu did not move. It was a small round head with thick hair, black and shiny as the feathers on the diving-ducks in the park across the river.

Or it might have been the head of a doll. A very fragile Chinese-china doll. Pratt walked round it to try and get a look at the face, the front of which was creamy-coloured with a nose so small it hardly made a bump, and leaf-shaped eyes with no eye-lashes. No, not leaf-shaped, pod-shaped, thought Pratt, and in each pod the blackest and most glossy berry which looked at the fish. The fish opened their mouths at the face in an anxious manner and waved their floaty tails about.

"What they telling you?" asked Pratt. "Friends of yours are they?"

Henry Wu said nothing.

"D'you want to go and see the diving-ducks in our park?"

Henry Wu said nothing.

"Think about it," said Pratt. "Next week. It's a good offer."

Henry Wu said nothing.

"Take it or leave it."

Pratt wondered for a moment if the Chinese boy was real. Maybe he was a sort of waxwork. If you gave him a push maybe he'd just tip over and fall on the floor. "Come on, Henry Wu," he said. "Let's hear what you think," and he gave the boy's shoulder a little shove.

And found himself lying on the floor with no memory of being put there. He was not at all hurt – just lying. And the Chinese boy was still sitting on his high stool looking at the fish.

Pandemonium was approaching along the passage and children of all kinds began to hurtle in. They all stopped in a huddle when they saw large Pratt spread out over the floor, and a teacher rushed forward. The Head Teacher and Jackson were there, too, at the back, and Jackson was looking surprised.

"Oh dear," said the teacher, "his mother taught him to fight in case he was bullied. She's a Black Belt in judo. She told us he was very good at it. Oh Henry – not again. This big boy wants to be kind to you."

"All I said," said Pratt, picking himself up, "Was that I'd take him to the diving-ducks in the park. What's more, I shall," he added, glaring at Henry Wu.

"Why bother?" said Jackson. They were on their way home. "He looks a wimp. He looks a rat. I don't call him unfortunate. I call him unpleasant."

"What was yours like?"

"Mine wasn't. She'd left. She was a fairground child. They're always moving on. The school seems a bit short of peculiar ones at the moment. I'll share Henry Wu the Great

84

Kung Fu with you if you like. You're going to need a bit of protection by the look of it."

But in the end Jackson didn't, for he was given an old lady's kitchen to paint and was soon spending his Wednesdays and all his free time in it, eating her cooking. Pratt set out the following week to the school alone and found Henry Wu waiting for him, muffled to just below the eyebrows in a fat grasshopper cocoon of bright red nylon padding.

"Come on," said Pratt and without looking to see if Henry followed, set out along the grim York Road to a bus-stop. Henry climbed on the bus behind him and sat some distance away, glaring at space.

"One and a half to the park," said Pratt, taking out a French grammar. They made an odd pair. Pratt put on dark glasses in case he met friends.

It was January. The park was cold and dead. The grass was thin and muddy and full of puddly places and nobody in the world could feel the better for seeing a blade of it. Plants were sticks. There were no birds yet about the trees, and the water in the lake and round the little island was heavy and dark and still, like forgotten soup.

The kiosk café was shut up. The metal tables and chairs of summer were stacked inside and the Coke machine was empty. Pigeons walked near the kiosk, round and round on the cracked tarmac. They were as dirty and colourless as everything else but Henry looked at them closely as they clustered round his feet. One bounced off the ground and landed on his head.

Henry did not laugh or cry out or jump, but stood.

"Hey, knock that off. It's filthy," shouted Pratt. "They're full of diseases. London pigeons. Look at their knuckles – all bleeding and rotten."

A large black-and-white magpie came strutting by and regarded Henry Wu with the pigeon on his head. The pigeon flew away. Henry Wu began to follow the magpie along the path.

"It's bad luck, one magpie," said Pratt, "One for sorrow, two for joy," and at once a second magpie appeared, walking behind. The Chinese boy walked in procession between the two magpies under the bare trees.

"Come on. It's time to go," said Pratt, feeling jealous. The magpies flew away, and they went to catch the bus.

Every Wednesday of that cold winter term, Pratt took Henry Wu to the park, walking up and down with his French book or his Science book open before him while Henry watched the birds and said nothing.

"Has he *never* said anything?" he asked the Head Teacher. "I suppose he talks Chinese at home?"

"No. He doesn't say a thing. There's someone keeping an eye on him of course. A Social Worker. But the parents don't seem to be unduly worried. His home is very Chinese, I believe. The doctors say that one day he should begin to speak, but maybe not for years. We have to be patient."

"Has he had some bad experiences? Is he a Boat Person?"

"No. He is just private. He is a village boy from China. Do you want to meet his family? You ought to. They ought to meet you, too. It will be interesting for you. Meeting Chinese."

"There are Chinese at our school."

"Millionaires' sons from Hong Kong I expect, with English as their first language. This will be more exciting. These people have chosen to come and live in England. They are immigrants."

"I'm going to meet some immigrants," said Pratt to Jackson. "D'you want to come?"

"No," said Jackson to Pratt, "I'm cleaning under Nellie's bed where she can't reach. And I'm teaching her to use a calculator."

"Isn't she a bit old for a calculator?"

"She likes it. Isn't it *em*igrants?"

"No, immigrants. Immigrants come *in* to a country."

"Why isn't it innigrants then?"

"I don't know. Latin I expect if you look it up. Emigrants are people who go out of a country."

"Well, haven't these Chinese come out of a country? As well as come in to a country? They're emigrants and immigrants. They don't know whether they're coming or going. Perhaps that's what's the matter with Henry Wu."

"Henry's not an innigrant. He's a *ninny*grant. Or just plain *innigrant*. I'm sick of him if you want to know. It's a waste of time, my Social Work. At least you get some good food out of yours. You've started her cooking again. And you're teaching her about machines."

"Your Chinese will know about machines. I shouldn't touch the food, though, if you go to them. It won't be like a Take-away."

"D'you want to come?"

"No thanks. See you."

"Candlelight Mansions," said the Social Worker. "Here we are. Twelfth floor and the lifts won't be working. I hope you're fit."

They climbed the concrete stairs. Rubbish lay about. People had scrawled ugly things on the walls. On every floor the lift had a board saying out of order hung across it with chains. Most of the chains were broken, too, so that the boards hung crooked. All was silent.

Then, as they walked more slowly up the final flights of stairs, the silence ceased. Sounds began to be threaded into it; thin, busy sounds that became more persistent as they turned at the twelfth landing and met a fluttery excited chorus. Across the narrow space were huge heaps. Bundles and crates and boxes were stacked high under tarpaulins with only the narrowest of alleys to lead up to the splintery front door of Henry Wu's flat. A second door of diamonds of metal was fastened across this. Nailed to the wall, on top of all the bundles were two big makeshift bird cages like sideways chicken-houses and inside them dozens of birds – red and blue and green and yellow making as much noise as a school playground.

"Oh dear," said the Social Worker, "Here we go again. The Council got them all moved once but the Wus just put them back. They pretend they don't understand. Good afternoon, Mrs Wu."

A beautiful, flat Chinese woman had come to the door and stood behind the metal diamonds. She did not look in the least like a Black Belt in judo. She was very thin and small and wore bedroom slippers, a satin dress and three cardigans. She bowed.

"I've just called for a chat and to bring you Henry's kind friend who is trying to help him."

Mrs Wu took out a key and then clattered back the metal gate and smiled and bowed a great deal and you couldn't tell what she was thinking. From the flat behind her there arose the most terrible noise of wailing, screeching and whirring, and Pratt thought that Jackson had been right about machines. A smell wafted out, too. A sweetish, dryish, spicy smell which sent a long thrill down Pratt's spine. It smelled of far, far away.

"You have a great many belongings out here," said the Social Worker climbing over a great many more as they made their way down the passage into the living-room. In the living-room were more again, and an enormous Chinese family wearing many layers of clothes and sitting sewing among electric fires. Two electric sewing-machines whizzed and a tape of Chinese music plinked and wailed, full-tilt. Another, different tape wailed back through the open kitchen door where an old lady was gazing into steaming pans on a stove. There were several bird cages hanging from hooks, a fish tank by the window and rat-like object looking out from a bundle of hay in a cage. It had one eye half-shut as if it had a headache. Henry Wu was regarding this rat.

The rest of the family all fell silent, rose to their feet and bowed. "Hello Henry," said Pratt, but Henry did not look round, even when his mother turned her sweet face on him and sang out a tremendous Chinese torrent.

Tea came in glasses. Pratt sat and drank his as the Social Worker talked to Mrs Wu and the other ladies, and a small fat Chinese gentleman, making little silk buttons without even having to watch his hands, watched Pratt. After a time he shouted something and a girl came carrying a plate. On the plate were small grey eggs with a skin on them. She held them out to Pratt.

"Hwile," said the Chinese gentleman, his needle stitching like magic. "Kwile."

"Oh yes," said Pratt. (Whale?)

"Eat. Eat."

"I'm not very ... "

But the Social Worker glared. "Quail," she said.

"Eggs don't agree ... " said Pratt. (Aren't quails snakes?) He imagined a tiny young snake curled inside each egg. I'd rather die, he thought, and saw that for the first time Henry Wu was looking at him from his corner. So was the rat.

So were the fish, the birds, Mrs Wu, the fat gentleman and all the assorted aunts. He ate the egg which went down glup, like an oval leather pill. Everyone smiled and nodded and the plate was offered again.

He ate another egg and thought, two snakes. They'll breed. I will die. He took a great swig of tea and smiled faintly. Everyone in the room then, except the rat, the fish and Henry, began to laugh and twitter and talk. The old woman slipper-sloppered in from the kitchen bringing more things to eat in dolls' bowls. They were filled with little chippy things and spicy, hot juicy bits. She pushed them at Pratt. "Go on," said the Social Worker. "Live dangerously."

Pratt ate. Slowly at first. It was delicious. "It's not a bit like the Take-Away," he said, eating faster. This made the Chinese laugh. "Take-Away, Take-Away," they said.

"Sweet-and-Sour," said Mrs Wu. "Not like Sweet-and-Sour," and everyone made tut-tutting noises which meant, "I should just hope not." Mrs Wu then gave Pratt a good-luck charm made of brass and nodded at him as if she admired him.

"She's thanking you for taking Henry out," said the Social Worker as they went down all the stairs again.

"She probably thinks I'm a lunatic," said Pratt, "Taking Henry out. Much good it's done."

"You don't know yet."

"Well, he's not exactly talking is he? Or doing anything. He's probably loopy. She probably thinks I'm loopy, too."

"She wouldn't let you look after him if she thought you were loopy."

"Maybe she wants rid of him. She's hoping I'll kidnap him. I'm not looking after him any more if he can't get up and say hello. Or even smile. After all those terrible afternoons. Well, I've got exams next term. I've got no time. I'll have to think of myself all day and every day from now on, thank goodness."

And the next term it was so. Pratt gave never a thought to Henry Wu except sometimes when the birds began to be seen about the school gardens again and to swoop under the eaves of the chapel. Swallows, he thought, immigrants. And he remembered him when his parents took him out to a Chinese restaurant on his birthday.

"Oh no – not those," he said.

"They are the greatest Chinese treat you can have," said his father. "Quails' eggs."

"Aren't they serpents?"

"Serpents? Don't you learn *any* general knowledge at that school? They're birds' eggs. Have some Sweet-and-Sour."

"The Chinese don't have Sweet-and-Sour. It was made up for the tourists."

"Really? Where did you hear that?"

"My Social Work."

* * *

The exams came and went as exams do and Pratt felt light-headed and light-hearted. He came out of the last one with Jackson and said, "Whee – let's go and look at the river."

"I feel great. Do you?" he said.

Jackson said he felt terrible. He'd failed everything. He'd spent too much time spring-cleaning old Nellie. He knew he had.

"I expect I've failed, too," said Pratt, but he felt he hadn't. The exams had been easy. He felt very comfortable and pleased with himself and watched the oily river sidle by, this way and that way, slopping up against the arches of the bridge, splashy from the barges. "What shall we do?" he asked Jackson. "Shall we go on the river?"

"I'd better go over and see if old Nellie's in," said Jackson. "I promised. Sorry. You go."

Pratt stood for a while and the old lady with the shopping-trolley went by. "Lolling about," she said.

"I'm sorry about your flour," said Pratt. Filled with happiness because the exams were over he felt he ought to be nice to the woman.

But she hurried on. Pratt watched her crossing the bridge and found his feet following. He made for Candlelight Mansions.

"Does Henry want to come to the park?" he asked a little girl who peered through the diamonds. Her face was like a white violet and her fringe was flimsy as a paint-brush. There was a kerfuffle behind her and Mrs Wu came forward to usher him inside.

If I go in it'll be quails' eggs and hours of bowing, thought Pratt. "I'll wait here," he said firmly. Mrs Wu disappeared and after a time Henry was produced, again muffled to the nose in the scarlet padding.

"It's pretty warm out," said Pratt, but Mrs Wu only nodded and smiled.

In the park Pratt felt lost without a book and Henry marched wordlessly, as far ahead as possible. The ice-cream kiosk was open now and people sitting on the metal chairs. Pigeons clustered round them in flustery clouds.

"Horrible," said Pratt, catching up with Henry. "Rats with wings. I'll get you a Coke but we'll drink it over there by the grass – hey! Where you going?"

Henry, not stopping for the pigeons, was away to the slope of green grass that led down to the water. On the grass and all over the water was a multitude of birds and all the ducks of the park, diving-ducks and pelicans and geese and dab-chicks and water-hens and mallards. Old ducks remembering and new little ducks being shown the summer for the first time. Some of the new ducks were so new they were still covered with fluff – white fluff, fawn fluff, yellow fluff and even black fluff, like decorations on a hat. The proud parent ducks had large V's of water rippling out behind them and small V's rippled behind all the following babies. Henry Wu stood still.

Then round the island on the lake there came a huge, drifting meringue.

It was followed by another, but this one had a long neck sweeping up from it with a proud head on the end and a brilliant orange beak and two black nostrils, the shape of Henry Wu's eyes.

The first meringue swelled and fluffed itself and a tall neck and wonderful head emerged from that one, too.

Suddenly Henry pointed a short padded arm at these amazing things and, keeping it stiff, turned his face up to Pratt and looked at him very intently.

"Swan," said Pratt. "They're swans. They're all right, aren't they? Hey – but don't do that. They're not so all right that you ought to get near them."

"Get that boy back," shouted a man. "They'll knock him down. They're fierce, them two."

"Nasty things, swans," said someone else.

But Henry was off, over the little green hooped fence, running at the swans as they stepped out of the water on their black macintosh feet and started up the slope towards him.

They lowered their necks and began to hiss. They opened their great wings.

"Oh help," said Pratt

"It's all right," said the man. "I'm the Warden. I'll get him. Skin him alive, too, if they don't do it first," and he ran down the slope.

But the swans did not skin Henry Wu alive. As he ran right up to them they stopped. They turned their heads away as if they were thinking. They shifted from one big black leathery foot to another and stopped hissing. Then they opened their wings wider still and dropped them gently and carefully back in place. They had a purple band round each left leg. One said 888. White swans, purple band, orange beaks, red Henry Wu, all on the green grass with the water and the willows about them, all sparkling and swaying.

"Bless him – isn't that nice now?" said the crowd, as the Warden of the swans gathered up Henry and brought him back under his arm.

"You'll get eaten one day," said the Warden, "You'll go getting yourself harmed," but he seemed less angry than he might.

On the way home Henry did not look at Pratt but sat with him on the long seat just inside the bus. It was a seat for three people and Henry sat as far away as possible. But it was the same seat.

Then Pratt went on his summer holidays and when he came back the exam results were out and they were not marvellous. He stuffed miserably about in the house. When Jackson called – Jackson had done rather well – he said that he was busy, which he wasn't.

But he made himself busy the next term, stodging glumly along, and took the exams all over again.

"Aren't you going to see your Chinese Demon any more?" asked Jackson afterwards. "Come and meet old Nellie."

"No thanks."

"She says to bring you."

"No thanks."

But when the results came out this time, they were very good. He had more than passed.

Pratt said, "How's Nellie?"

"Oh fine. Much better tempered."

"Was she bad tempered? You never said."

"How's Henry Wu? Did you ever get him talking?"

"No. He was loopy."

But it was a fine frosty day and the sun for the moment was shining and Pratt went to the park and over the grass to the lakeside where one of the swans came sliding around the island and paddled about on the slope, marking time and looking at him.

It dazzled. The band round his leg said 887. "Where's your husband?" said Pratt. "Or wife or whatever? Are you hungry or something?"

The sun went in and the bare trees rattled. The swan looked a bit lonely and he thought he might go and get it some bread. Instead he took a bus back over the bridge and went to Candlelight Mansions.

They've probably forgotten me, he thought as he rang the bell. The bundles and the bird cages had gone from the landing. He rattled the steel mesh. They've probably moved, he thought. They'll have gone back to China.

But he was welcomed like a son.

"Can I take Henry out?"

Bowings, grinnings, buttonings-up of Henry who had not grown one millimetre.

"Where's the rat?" Pratt asked.

"Nwee-sance," said Mrs Wu.

"Neeoo-sance," said the fat gentleman. "Nee-oosance. Council told them go."

But the flat was now a jungle of floating paper-kites and plants with scarlet dragons flying about in them, mixed with Father Christmases, Baby Jesuses and strings of Christmas tinsel. In the kitchen the old lady stirred the pots to a radio playing *Oh Come All Ye Faithful*. Henry, seeing everyone talking together sat down under a sewing-machine.

"Has he said anything yet?" asked Pratt, eating juicy bits with chopsticks. Everyone watched the juicy bits falling off the chopsticks and laughed. Now and then, when anything reached his mouth successfully, they congratulated him. They ignored the question, which meant that Henry had not.

It was cold in the street and very cold as they stood at the bus stop. Pratt had forgotten that the days were now so short, and already it was beginning to get dark. Far too late to go to the park, he thought. The bus was cold, too, and dirty, and all the people looked as if they'd like to be warm at home in bed. "Come on – we'll go upstairs and sit in the front," said Pratt and they looked down on the dreary York Road with all its little half-alive shops and, now and then, a string of coloured Christmas lights across it with most of the bulbs broken or missing. Some shops had spray-snowflakes squirted on the windows. It looked like cleaning-fluid someone had forgotten to wash off. Real snowflakes were beginning to fall and looked even dingier than the shop-window ones.

I should have taken him over the river to see some real Christmas lights in Regent Street, thought Pratt. There's nothing over here.

But there came a bang.

A sort of rushing, blustering, flapping before the eyes.

The glass in the window in front of them rattled like an earthquake and something fell down in front of the bus.

There were screeching brakes and shouting people and Pratt and Henry were flung forward on to the floor.

As they picked themselves up they saw people running into the road below. "Something fell out of the sky," said Pratt to Henry Wu. "Something big. Like a person. Come on – we've got to get out."

But it was not a person. It was a swan that sat heavy and

large and streaked with a dark mark across its trailing wings in the very middle of the road.

"Swan, swan – it's a swan!" Everybody was shouting. "It's killed itself. It's dead. Frozen dead with fright."

"It hit a wire," said someone else – it was the woman with the shopping trolley – "I saw it. An overhead-wire from the lights. They oughtn't to be allowed. They're not worth it. They could have electrocuted that bus."

"It's killed it, anyway," said Jackson, who seemed to be with her. "It's stone dead."

But the swan was not dead. Suddenly it decided it was not. It heaved up its head and wings and lollopped itself to the side of the road and flopped down again, looking round slowly, with stunned wonder, opening and shutting its orange beak, though with never a sound.

"It was migrating," said the man from a chip-shop.

"Swans don't migrate, they stay put," said a man from a laundry.

"Anyone'd migrate this weather," said a man selling whelks and eels. "Look, it's got a number on it. It's from the park. Look, it's put itself all tidy on the yellow line."

"Out of the way," said a policeman. "Now then. Stand aside. We'll want a basket." A laundry-basket was brought and someone lent the policeman a strong pair of gloves.

"Clear a space," he said and approached the swan which proved it was not dead by landing the policeman a thwacking blow with its wing.

"Have to be shot," said a dismal man from a bike-shop. "Well, it's no chicken."

"Course it's no chicken," said the woman with the trolley. "If it was a chicken it'd be coming home with me and a bag of chips."

And then a girl with purple hair began to shriek and scream because she didn't believe in eating animals, which included birds.

"Anyway, all swans belong to the Queen," said the trolley-lady. "I heard it on Gardener's Question Time."

"I'm going crazy," said the policeman who had withdrawn to a little distance to talk into his radio-set. "If they all belong to the Queen I hope she'll come and collect this one. I'm not sure I can. Move along now. We have to keep the traffic moving. We can't hold up London for a swan."

One or two cars sidled by, but otherwise nobody moved. It was a strange thing. In the middle of the dead dark day and the dead dark street sat the open laundry basket and the shining, mute bird with its angel feathers. The road fell quiet.

Then Henry Wu stepped foward, small inside his padding, and put short arms round the bulk of the swan's back and lifted it lightly into the basket where it fluffed up its feathers like rising bread and gazed round proudly at the people.

"Heaven on high!" said everyone. "The weight!"

"His mother's a Black Belt," said Pratt proudly.

"That Chinese'll have to be washed," said the trolley-lady. "They'd better both come home with us, Jackson, and I'll give them their tea."

But Pratt and Henry did not go home with old Nellie on that occasion because the policemen asked them to go back to the station with him and the swan. If Henry would be so kind as to assist him, he said. And Henry stroked the swan's docile head twice and then folded it down with its neck behind it – and a big strong neck it was, though very arrangeable – and quickly put down the lid.

The Park Warden came to the police station and he and Henry and Pratt and the swan then went on to the park, where the swan took to the water like a whirlwind and faded into the dark.

"Off you go, 888," said the Warden. "There's your missus to meet you. You wouldn't have seen her again if you'd not dropped among friends."

"They can't take off, you see," he said to the two boys, "Except on water. They're like the old sea-planes."

Pratt watched the two white shapes fade with the day.

"They're strange altogether, swans," said the Warden. "Quite silent!"

"Is it true they sing when they're dying?" asked Pratt. "I read it. In poetry."

"Well, that one's not dying then," said the Warden. "Gone without a sound. It's funny – most living creatures make some sort of noise to show they're happy. Goodbye, Henry. There'll be a job for you with creatures one day. I dare say when you grow up you'll get my job. You have the touch."

On the bus back over the bridge to Candlelight Mansions Henry sat down next to Pratt on a double seat and staring in front of him said in a high, clear Chinese-English voice, "Hwan."

"Hwan," he said. "Hwan, hwan, hwan, swan. Swan, swan, SWAN," until Pratt had to say, "Shut up Henry or they'll think you're loopy."

GROUNDLINGS

"Is she there?"

"Yes, she's there."

First thing you ever do is look to see if she's there. Bundle of clothes in the dark, pressed up close beside the ticket-office. She's always the same, lying prone on a length of black macintosh. Nothing much around her, not even a thermos. Never like the rest of us with camp-stool, rugs and books. I've never seen her with a book, not in nearly forty years.

I've known old Aggie Batt in theatre queues all of thirty-five years, anyway. She looks no different from the 1945 season at The New. Oh my – Olivier, Gielgud, Guinness! Richardson's *Cyrano*! The Old Vic – but it was in St Martin's Lane then. All London was full of theatres that were still part of war-time, turned into offices, or shells with the daylight shining through, or rubble with the daisies growing.

There was good standing-room at St Martin's Lane. For a shilling you could stand all down the side aisles, leaning your shoulder against the wall. They didn't let you sit down, even for *Anthony and Cleopatra* or *Hamlet* in its entirety. "Eternity" the actors used to call it, but I don't think we ever did. If you slid down on your haunches, usherettes came along and hissed at you to stand up because of fire regula-tions. Fire in the loins. And they didn't let you take your shoes off because of being alongside all the people in the stalls who had paid good money. I don't know why the stalls didn't complain anyway, all the students in huge hairy duffles standing down the side-aisles three feet away from them; but they didn't. It was just after the War when there was still good-temper about. Students were ever so quiet then. Shy. You wouldn't believe. Ever so thin and grey-looking. Well, it was all the poor food we'd had wasn't it? Even bread on coupons. But, oh it was a wonderful year that, '45 – '46, first term at college for me, all the theatres getting going, all the actors coming back, new plays starting and the great big expensive yelling American musicals. After all the bombed indoor years.

I don't think I was ever so hungry as I was then – much worse than in the war. If you went to an evening performance you missed college-dinner, as well as the last bus, and never a penny over for a sandwich at a Lyons corner house. Two-mile walk home, the last bit through Regent's Park at midnight, but nobody worried. No muggers. We went dreaming home, stage-struck, Shakespeare-struck, Annie-get-your-Gun struck. Slaughtering over. We'd won. First things first now. You should have seen Olivier's Mr Puff.

Not that she – Aggie Batt, we christened her – ever was to be seen queuing for the American musicals or even for the Sheridan. It was Shakespeare for Aggie Batt, Shakespeare then and Shakespeare now. Shakespeare all the way. There was never a Shakespeare night she wasn't there.

That's to say she was there every night that I and my friends were there, and between us all we didn't miss much. And Aggie B. was always at the head of the queue as she was until this very year.

We laughed at her. She wore a balaclava helmet and men's socks and grey gloves that looked made out of wire, and shiny brown trousers with flies, and a queer jacket, double-breasted. Her face was sharp and disagreeable with a tight little mouth. She had small hard eyes. She looked a bit mad and she hasn't changed. She has grown no madder. She is just the same. A *little* mad. A bit bonkers.

I suppose her face is older now. It must be. It must have more lines on it. It must be more leathery. But I can't say that I can tell. I mean, you don't if it's someone you're used to seeing year in, year out, like family. My own face strikes me as being no different really, until I see the photographs. I went to an old-students' reunion once and it was terrible. Embarrassing. Most of us, if we recognised one another, just yattered on with fixed smiles and slunk off home. But that's by the way.

Aggie Batt is ageless. Ageless as the years roll on and the theatre-queues change and become stream-lined and organised and tickets a matter for scientific pre-plotting. In her way she is a famous figure, a well-known part of the London theatre scene. I mean of course well-known to the groundlings, the queuers, not to the people who only go to the theatre if they can get a good seat. She is there repeatedly, at every production. After a first-night if you don't see her in the queue for the second night you know there must be something very wrong. A performance at the National or the Old Vic or the Barbican will have to be abysmal if she's not present then, and many times more. She is a comfort, Aggie Batt, disdaining time. She is a symbol. She is homage. When we see her we grin. We say "There's Aggie" but we are really saying "There's one of us, the best of us." Through Aggie Batt we know our tribe.

I've often tried to speak to Aggie Batt but it's not easy. For all the notice she's taken of me all these years I might be invisible. It's probably because I'm not serious enough. At the beginning, when I was eighteen, I was just one of a gaggle of girls – a first-year student. I'm not that exclusive about Shakespeare you see, and never was. I like to go to everything. As far as I'm concerned it's the only way to keep going, the theatre. Any theatre. I spend a lot of money but I don't have time as my husband says to spend money on much else, and I've got money now, having married it. I'm a very comfortable theatre-goer. I have a fur-lined mac from Harrods and a huge great tartan coat from Aquascutum. I still get my tickets mostly through the theatre-queue though, because (a) you get good seats (b) you get good company and (c) it's home.

More home than home. I don't get the same chance to talk

at home. I very much like nattering on. It's a pity that these days the queue has changed a bit. There are a lot of people now not very talkative or who want to sleep. People are tireder nowadays, especially men. Well, I'm nearly sixty now. They don't notice me.

Aggie Batt doesn't sleep much. She lies there on her black macintosh sheet with her eyes open. Whatever I talk about she scarcely blinks.

The first hour of queuing, if it's a popular production – say a Hopkins *Lear* or a new *Hamlet* – Piggot-Smith or Roger Rees – the queue will start to collect while it's still dark. If it's winter it will be still the deep dark. For the first hour's queueing she'll be lying back to the road, her face up against the plate-glass (if it's the National) like an Arab in a Gulf airport in a sandstorm. In winter all the lights are out along the river – only the occasional window shining high up in the Shell building and the odd street-lamp on the bridge. As the dawn comes up somebody, somewhere switches on long necklaces of light-bulbs, pink and gold, all along the riverside terraces. They come on as it gets light. An eccentric idea. You'll notice then, suddenly, – Aggie Batt moves very quietly – that she's sitting with her knees drawn up in front of her, eating biscuits out of a bag and staring straight ahead. She'll get up then and pace about a bit, flexing her fingers in the wire gloves, her nose sticking out sharp from the balaclava if it's that sort of day. In summer it's a scarf. She'll go off somewhere – I suppose to the Ladies at Waterloo Station – and come back and stand in profile to the river. It's a tense, fierce profile. Richard III. The Scottish King. Nothing very friendly about it. She'll stand maybe half an hour like this. Then she'll turn toward the bridge and watch The Great Procession.

I've rather stopped watching the Procession now, after so many years. It is the procession of the people of South London that takes place Monday to Friday with as great punctuality as the changing of the guard at Buckingham

102

Palace. It is the procession that floods across Waterloo Bridge from the Station, across the river to work. It is a very fine sight. It is an army of silently tramping, non-conversing, face-forward, jerking, walking, trotting, running ants, heads held tense, hands hard-gripping on cases, umbrellas, newspapers, the coming day. It continues, a steady flow, for the best part of two hours, dwindling off at just after ten o'clock. It is the march of the disciplined, the bread-winners, the money-grubbers, the money-needers, often the dead. Over the Bridge they tramp, south to north, in to the stomach of London. They don't look over their shoulder and down or they would see us, their opposites, as in a mediaeval diptych of heaven and hell – or hell and heaven: the motley bundles of the theatre-queuers looking upwards and over at them as we blink with sleep. Us, the pleasure-lovers, the pleasure-seekers, the unrepentant from across the wide world, the creatures of high holiday. Gazing and munching and blinking we sit – big loose Australians, intellectual Indians, serious Americans, antiseptic Japanese and all the mongrel English, including me in fur or plaid, the fastidious Yorkshire lad with the walk-way (another regular) and the lady with the diamond earrings and the New York accent and the Harrods deck-chair, reading a famous critic on The Scottish Play. Once there was even the critic himself. He drove right up beside us in a Rolls-Royce. He got out and locked it – you can park right down on the river-side if it's before eight o'clock in the morning – and joined the queue. He didn't speak (like Aggie Batt) even when I offered him a sandwich. He just smiled politely. He was deep in something to do with a First Folio.

I remember that I wanted to tell someone that there was someone famous and he was reading about First Folios and I went back to my place again – I'd been stretching my legs – near the top of the queue. Then I went actually to the very top of the queue and I said to Aggie Batt, "Look who's there. He's reading about First Folios," and – it's one of the very few times in all these years I've heard her speak – she said, "Very fragmented."

What can you say to that? Did she mean that the FF (it was *Ant. and Cle.*) was very fragmented? Did she mean that this critic was very fragmented? Or what I said was not cogent? That's what the remark used to be at the end of many of my Shakespeare essays – "Not cogent." Maybe she did think that the play was very fragmented – I know I do. I've often thought you could cut a lot of those little bitty scenes at the end. Everyone – actors, audience – are too tired for them by then. Everybody knows, even if they haven't read the play they know, that everyone's having to reserve strength for the death scenes, especially Anthony. Cleopatra – well after the asp it's all quite quiet for her. She just has to sit dead and be carried out. The asp must be rather a relief. I'd forgotten all the notes I had on it once but I think they were on this Aggie Batt line of argument, and I was grateful to her, for when I'd bought my ticket at ten o'clock – I always stand to one side while I check my seat-number and so on, even if the rest of the queue behind me has to step over my blankets – the great man looked at me, and I was able to say, "I see you are reading from the First Folio, Sir. It's very fragmented isn't it?" He seemed to be quite surprised.

You'll probably have seen Aggie Batt in the audience many a time. She doesn't look at all as she does in the queue in the morning. Oh dear me no. She wears a black dress up to the neck, long in the arms, and her hair that is invisible under the balaclava turns out to be long and fine. From the morning appearance you'd expect what used to be called The Eton Crop – very mannish and coarse, like metal, the kind that ought to clatter when you run your hand through it. Julius Caesar hair. Nothing of the sort. It is light and downy and thin so that you can almost see the scalp through and it's not so much white as the colour of light, though I'm not putting this very well.

Oh and dear me, she is thin. Through the black dress you

can see her old shoulder-blades sticking out at the back and her collar-bones at the front. She has a long shawl affair that floats about – ancient – and when she lets it go loose you can see her hip bones and her stomach a hollow below them. She could be Pavlova in extremis except for oh dear, her legs! Her legs are old bits of twig. She wears very old, cracked, shoes with broad black ribbons tied in bows, stockings with ladders, and often a pair of socks.

She's nearly always in the same seat – G25. You've seen her. Every time you've been to a London Shakespeare. You've sat next to her perhaps. It's an old joke in the queue, G25: someone saying that they'll get to the queue twenty-four hours early so they can get G25 to see what she'd do without it: see if she'd drop dead. I didn't think anything of him for saying it.

She never buys a programme, that's another thing. She doesn't seem to need one. There's a number of people don't, of course. I remember when I was young I didn't. It was a snob thing. I used to take the text instead, and a torch, and follow with my finger. It was very helpful for exams, though if there was a row of us doing it people round about got tetchy. We were like glow-worms. In those days I didn't need a programme anyway because I knew who everyone was and which was playing what. I know most of them now, but not like Aggie Batt, who I suppose breathes them all in by osmosis. As I say, she never has a book with her, she's not one for a text. It's the performance for her. It's him. Himself. William the Man she comes for. The play she wants. The living thing in action. That's what the walk-way boy says. He seldom speaks either, but he sits near her often and seems to have picked things up from her.

He says she lives in North London behind Kings Cross and walks everywhere. She even walks there and back to the Barbican – five miles each way. She walks there and back in the morning for the ticket and there and back in the evening for the performance. Isn't she afraid of walking about the empty Kings Cross streets so late at night? No. She carries in her purse the exact money for her ticket plus thirty-five p. for a cup of tea; and her pension book.

But she can't be utterly poor. Walk-way boy says she's travelled. Seen *Hamlet* in Denmark. Been to Shakespeare Festivals in Berlin. I asked her what she thought of Berlin and it was one of her answering days and she said "Professors of Shakespeare look like steel rats." One day I bought her a pie. She seemed pleased. It was just a pie from the stall under the station arches but she ate it with hunger and nodded at me and even answered the question I asked her while I was gathering up her rubbish. This I have to keep doing for she surrounds herself with quite a lot of it. I asked her who was her favourite character in Shakespeare and she said Enobarbus. I asked her which was her favourite play and she said "*The Winter's Tale*, but it's getting late for it now."

I've seen her in a *Winter's Tale* queue several times so I didn't know what she meant. I thought that maybe her memory was slipping and she was forgetting what she had seen. Not that that has ever seemed to me such a great deprivation. If you lose your memory you can experience things again as if they were new, like when you were young.

Well no. Never really like that.

Next *Winter's Tale* I told myself I'd take her a bunch of flowers. I don't suppose anyone ever gave Aggie Batt flowers. Years and years ago there was a young man used to be in the queue. Oh, he was about nineteen I'd think and she must then have been nearly forty. They used to go off together after an hour or two's queueing, leaving the black mac. They used to sit side by side on the black mac. He I remember used to leave a pair of yellow leather gloves on it to keep their places. He had that ripply, goldielocks hair you see sometimes on young men and a very soft mouth and gently moving hips. You didn't comment in those days but you sniggered. Somehow though I never sniggered.

He stopped being around after a while. One of the sniggerers heard he'd run off to be a ballet-dancer. Aggie Batt looked madder then, her face more severe. She began to carry a walking-stick and twirl it about. After I was married, my husband sometimes came to join the theatre queue with me – just at first. One day we arrived very early and we saw the poor old bundle, with the walking stick alongside, on the black mac. "Good God, what's that? Who's that poor old man?"

"Sssh, it's Aggie Batt."

He looked down the queue and said "Looks like a string of winos, but my word! The one at the top!"

My husband's full of quips. Once when I was late home from a seven-hour stint of the *Henrys* he'd put my mail out on the hall-stand re-directed, "Not known at this address. Try The National Theatre." But he wouldn't be bothered with jokes about Aggie Batt.

And why am I writing all this? What is so special about her? After all, she's dead now. The London theatre is going along perfectly well without her. There has been no obituary and she won't ever be mentioned in any memoir. She's not as far as I know ever been referred to in a theatre column or theatre magazine or been interviewed on television. I don't think she ever heard of television. What was she? An interesting psychiatric subject for discussion: a woman with a Shakespeare fixation. That is all.

Well, it is not all. I am writing down all that I know now about her because it is not all, and because of the wonderful thing that happened the day she died, and if you don't believe a word of it, what do I care? Shakespeare's plots were unbelievable. Larger than life. When people say to me, "Oh, I say – another story larger than life" I say to myself, think of Shakespeare. Think for example of the story of *The Winter's Tale*, and I say, "Things may be larger than your life but they are not larger than mine."

Well, it was to be the first night of what promised to be a marvellous *Winter's Tale*. The pre-view notices had been

non-pareils. The agency tickets had been sold out weeks
before. We had read already in all the papers of the wonderful, ice-bound Act One and the blooming and blossoming
dizzy Spring in store for us in Act Two: the songs and the
sheep-shearing, the frolic, then the regeneration, the triumph
over wickedness and death at the end. Huge portraits of the
players were plastered against the glass sides of the National:
pictures of yokels and bears, statues and queens and sages,
and Perdita and her princeling – the hopes of the world.

I decided that to be sure of a seat I must leave home about
5.30 a.m. and drive to London in the car. I didn't tell anyone
at home that I was going so early because there's opposition
nowadays on account of my leg and the time I didn't see the
Sutton roundabout.

I crept out of the house and it was already light – a warm,
Spring morning. All the birds of Tadworth making a racket
like Illyria. I stood for a moment thinking how much I love
Tadworth. All the birds, and so easy for the theatre. I thought
how much more musical suburban birds are than country ones
and wondered what the Southwark birds had been like in
Shakespeare's time. Thinking of Shakespeare and *Winter's
Tale* I went round to our garden at the back to pick Aggie
some flowers. There were some lovely primroses and still
some nice daffs, though some had gone a bit brown-papery, a
few primulas and six little irises. We've a nice garden. I put
them in a plastic bag with a bit of blue rue we have by the gate
and stowed them in the glove compartment and roared off
down the drive trying not to look in case any angry heads were
sticking out of bedroom windows. My daughter is a light
sleeper and not just now my friend. I imagined her furious
face. "For goodness *sake*! Adolescent! Immature! Sitting
with students!" and so on. My daughter is in Management
Consultancy although I called her Cordelia. She doesn't
understand.

It was difficult parking the car that morning. Someone had
forgotten to take the chain down from across the theatre

108

forecourt and I had to go half-way to Southwark to the car-park where you take a ticket from a sleepy man in a box and the surface is like craters of the moon. It can't have been worse in Shakespeare's time. Great puddles. I set off walking back. Ten minutes.

That can make all the difference from being number twenty and number thirty in the queue. Each person in the queue for tickets sold on day of performance is allowed two tickets. There are only forty tickets altogether unless there are returns, and there are unlikely to be returns for a First Night, so ten minutes can mean defeat.

So I went pounding along to the National, past the head of the queue where of course lay Aggie Batt, fast asleep, and for some reason feet foremost today, lying at right-angles to the glass wall, her head below the enormous chin of Edward Woodward picked out in purple. Even she wasn't first in the queue for this performance. There was a man ahead of her leaning against the glass, reading, and then the Yorkshire walk-way boy sitting cross-legged, staring ahead, numbed by the secret music under the ear-muffs. "Late," I called out, but neither the man nor the boy nor Aggie Batt made any sign. I went to the end of the line and dumped my cushion and blankets and stood out from the wall – we all sit under a wide cement awning which shields us from the rain – very different from the old days, humped in raincoats under umbrellas on little battered stools. I counted back and I was number 45. So I wasn't going to be lucky.

However, you never know. Miracles sometimes happen and other hopefuls were still gathering up behind me, think-ing likewise. I wrapped myself up and watched the Bridge. I slept a bit I think because it suddenly seemed much lighter and the people round about were beginning to eat things. I drank some coffee from my thermos and wished I'd brought a book. There were huge Germans on either side of me, fast asleep. Nobody to talk to.

Soon the day-light began to wane again as clouds came over

and rain began. Never say die, I thought and felt in my pockets for chocolate – then remembered the flowers I'd left behind in the glove-compartment, way down Pickle-Herring Street. I felt tired and my leg was jumping.

However – I put my thermos on the cushion to keep my place and set off back past the head of the queue. Aggie Batt had not stirred, neither had the leaning man (what strength of shin!) nor the walk-way boy. "Just going to the car," I called, but I'm like scenery. They didn't speak.

When I came back again with the flowers in the plastic bag I had an idea. I have never had this idea before. I have *never* asked, for it is not done – to ask someone buying only one ticket near the top of the queue if they'll buy their allowance of two and sell one back to you. The walk-way never buys more than a single ticket and neither of course does Aggie Batt, but asking her would be out of the question. It would mean sitting next to her through the play and chatting, which I knew she would never countenance. It would be like asking a nun to share her hassock or a fakir to shift over on his mat.

"S'okay," said the walk-way boy, lifting off a muff an inch. Little tinny sounds came out, like distant revels. He let it spring back in place and I sat beside him and took out my purse and counted the money. I felt dreadful, breaking the rules, and I said to the standing man, "I know him. He's a very – old friend. I've never done this before." I looked at Aggie but she was still asleep. Sleeping late. Peaceful. I took the flowers from the bag, bound them round with the elastic band from my sandwiches and the boy and the man watched.

I laid the flowers on Aggie Batt's chest for her to find when she woke. The boy paid no attention now but the man continued to watch. "It's because it's *Winter's Tale*," I said, "It's her favourite." Although he did not speak I knew that he found what I had done acceptable. I also knew that I need say no more and I went back to my place.

I am a garrulous woman. I suppose by now that's clear. I cannot help it. It is because I am not confident. I am not even confident about Shakespeare. I only got a Lower Second. I try to justify myself too much. I try to explain my hungry need for Shakespeare by trying to be learned about him – catching on to other people's stuff about First Folios and textuality and fragmentation and things not being cogent rather than just saying that when I am watching Shakespeare I am happier than at any other time. I knew as I sat down at the end of the queue again that I had no need to justify myself to that man and I felt young again. I felt rather as I had done long ago, when I was eighteen standing in the aisle at the New Theatre, famished, light-headed, looking forward. It was like falling in love.

Soon the necklaces of lights came on and the rain stopped, leaving big pools about on the concrete. A warm, quite summery breeze blew over us and I may have dropped off because all at once I noticed the welcome 9.45 a.m. signs of life inside the National's glass wall. The counter of the ticket-office was being dusted and a Hoover was being wheeled away, lights switched on.

There is a moment in the theatre queue and it is 9.59 a.m. With one accord, like the audience at Messiah with the lift of the baton for the Hallelujah Chorus, everyone rises to his feet. Everyone does a shuffling left turn and stands waiting. Hardly a sound. Then the man inside looks at his watch, comes out from his lair, undoes the bolts and opens the glass doors, and without pause the whole queue begins to flow forward, each person holding six or twelve pounds or a cheque-book like a talisman. The queue marches through and the whole thing is over in less than a quarter of an hour.

But not this morning, for when I reached the head of the queue, Aggie Batt had not got up. She lay there with her nose as sharp as a pen and the flowers on her chest.

The queue passed round her of course. As was right. I stayed with her, waiting for the walk-way boy to come with our tickets and when he did, he knelt down by her and took off his ear-muffs and began to undo her jacket and scarves.

111

The leaning man who'd been ahead of her had disappeared –
he wasn't a regular. He'd probably hardly noticed her, deep
in his book. The last tail-end of the queue reluctantly stepped
round her. A few stood lingering about in the forecourt,
looking towards us, before going away.

I told the boy to find someone quick, to get an ambulance,
but he said "No hurry. She's dead," and I felt her face and it
was ice-cold. "She's been dead for hours," he said, "I know.
I'm a hospital porter," and he went inside, slowly, to find a
telephone. "You'd think that man would have noticed," I
said, "Standing beside her all this time. He was ahead of her.
He must have been there when she arrived." "What man?"
said the boy, "There wasn't any man. She was head of the
queue."

When the ambulance had taken away what remained of
Aggie Batt, and the walk-way boy gone off to get us some
coffee, I put my ticket in my purse and went over towards the
river. I watched the great procession streaming over the
Bridge, swirling along like the water below. The people of
Shakespeare's parish.

DAMAGE

She terrified me. She looked like a fly. Threadwire arms and legs arranged all anyhow across a slatted seat in the Jardin Anglais: the lake cold and thrashing about against the quay, the wind squealing in the shrouds of the wintering boat-yard. Why should a fly terrify? How can a woman on a park bench be a fly? Something mingy about her. Bothersome. Unhealthy. Not poor – rich, rich. Look at her shoes! And all so small, and twisted sideways. Wearing black. Not young. Skinny. And sobbing, sobbing, sobbing.

January. Geneva. And, unusually for me, Geneva on Saturday. For years I have been coming to work in Geneva, flipping back and forth from London. I go to other places – Prague, Berlin, Lisbon, The Hague – but to Geneva mostly. I am a translator. I translate at international conferences and arbitrations, simultaneously with the spoken word. I have four languages and am in much demand. As the speaker spouts out the message from the podium I drink his words into my head and ears and fountain them out again, translated. Tensely but steadily, smoothly, almost unhesitatingly they flow out of my mouth on to a disc at the end of a microphone which is enclosed with me inside a glass bubble fitted over my desk.

My voice is transferred about the room to the ears of those delegates whose language I am speaking. It passes through holes in similar discs fitted to their ears by a band across the head. One day this will be thought very comical and antique. One day there will be a machine and not me beneath the bubble. Perhaps one day we shall all have our brains nipped about at birth and there will be one universal language. Later still there will be perhaps a miraculous speaking in tongues and our heads surrounded not by plastic ear-phones but by points of fire, and there shall be a new heaven and a new earth and fewer arguments. But, until the ultimate machine or the Apocalypse, they must have me, and those like me.

We sit in a row – four of us at this arbitration – along the foot of the stage, our lips constantly moving. I have no way of knowing which ones in the audience are listening to me and which to my colleagues. Delegates select their own channels. Once I translated into German for a whole morning not having been told that the German delegates had missed their plane, and my words, my tens of thousands of words, had been passing into air. Or rather they had never existed, as at the beginning of the world when volcanoes, tidal-waves, hurricanes happened in silence for want of an ear-drum against which to sound.

Once when I was young and frisky and new to my profession I used to long to take the microphone into my power, spread mischief. "Here is an important announcement. Her Majesty, Queen Elizabeth the Second of England, is filing a suit for divorce." "Mr Gorbachev, having recently contracted the AIDS virus, has announced his intention of seeking the comforts of the Russian Orthodox Church." "Nude bathing is to be allowed from tomorrow morning along the Swiss shore of Lake Léman. Delegates interested in forming bathing-parties should assemble by the Jardin Anglais at eight o'clock. In the buff." Heads would jerk. Mouths fall open. These things are dreams.

I plug on, hard at it, thinking only of words and words.

It is tiring, especially if the case is technical, has its own specialised vocabulary which has had to be worked up for weeks before a session begins and often revised during the hearing in the evenings.

By Friday afternoon at four o'clock I am always exhausted and try wherever I am to get home for the week-end. I have a pretty cottage in Putney, bought with my alimony. I have a very old father in South Wimbledon. On Sundays I go to see him, cook our lunch. He expects me, though he does not greet me. After lunch he sleeps, with the *Sunday Telegraph* over his face, while I wash up the dishes. In summer I mow his small lawn. In autumn I sweep up and burn the leaves from his trees. In winter I may bake him a cake. He is disappointed in me. He liked my husband.

I go back to Putney after tea – washing, ironing, hair, nails – and late at night or on Monday morning catch a plane that will have me attached to my discs again by ten-thirty their time, nine-thirty ours.

I am always put in good hotels. The very best – and this in Geneva means in one of the best hotels in the world. I am also, I suppose, well-paid, though not so especially well when you consider where the world would be without me. I am usually with the same group of translators, but it happens that we none of us talk much about such things as the pay. We are a curious breed and, though a breed, we do not stick together. Translators have little in common except the kink in the brain and the teaspoonful of heredity that has given us our eerie linguistic memory – though we ourselves find nothing eerie in it. It is simply the ability to sing in tune in different keys. A gift. We tend to be solitaries. Mynah birds. You seldom see Mynah birds roosting together.

At the end of each day's session we vanish separately from the chamber, each to his bough.

Mine is always the hotel – my bedroom, with its en-suite bathroom and sometimes sitting-room; its marbled basins, its coloured telephones – one even upon the bath – its clutches of lights. When I arrive at each new hotel I make solemn acknowledgement of all these, and of the presents: the soaps, the foam-baths, the shampoos, the bath-caps, the scents, the talcs, the bowl of fruit done up in thick transparent paper with the note saying 'Welcome', and, every night, the three round chocolates wrapped in silver paper on the pillow.

And six great fat white bath towels every day!

I pad across the fleecy carpet and open the fridge full of

drink – all the little bottles of spirits and liqueurs looking like free samples. I hardly drink, not even the frosted wine crammed in discreet half-bottles on the shelves below, ready for romance. I take it all out sometimes and look at it. And all the soft drinks and bags of nuts! Years of these treats now – ever since my husband left – but I've never grown used to such bounty. Such gifts – and nobody looking!

I lie back and gaze at the television. It is nondescript in every country but Britain, but I gaze. I yawn with langour. I twirl my naked foot. I play the switches at my bedside one after another – all the music channels. 'And when I leave,' I tell the ceiling, 'I don't even have to pay the bill.' I am thirty. It is my retarded area. My secret sin.

The big hotels I stay in differ very little from one another wherever they are and I am not very interested in what goes on outside them. Countries are countries. It's a small world. My time and money are given to my appearance. Concerts, theatres, dinners are expensive and there need to be two of you. So I work at my clothes, my figure, my skin. For health I walk about a little. I listen to my feet in their Gambazetti pumps making hollow clops about the lunch-time picture galleries. In Geneva, in the evenings, I walk in the Old Town, looking at the lighted shop-windows: spot-light, gold and diamond cluster, twenty yards of velvet back-cloth. I examine the *objets d'art* in the antique shops. They seldom change. They seem covered in golden dust.

The streets of Geneva are quiet at night exposing it for the little provincial town it is. At midnight on the wide deserted streets all that move are the jujube traffic-lights dotted here and there into the distance. The few people patiently waiting near them – the slowest-changing lights in the world: they seem always to be standing at red – cross over at last. Over they go, left-right.

People who walk alone in Geneva keep their eyes wide and unsmiling. Nobody touches. Ladies sit easily alone, or maybe two or three, very quiet. Very confident. There is gold about.

A good many necklaces, bracelets, watches. A great many rings. Always earrings. Always painted faces, however old. A formal city. Waiters – the emblems, the daemons of Geneva, cold, colourless, rich – keep their distance, watchful as policemen. At a loud voice or laugh they look sharply across.

Once or twice a year the waiters stand guard over the empty restaurants as the rest of the city pays to watch from its own streets the millions of dollars-worth of fireworks exploding over the lake in cascades of chrysanthemums, peacock-tails, palms. These are greeted with a drifting, respectful murmur, a shifting of feet, a ripple of milk-and-water clapping, and never a coarse hurrah. Everything is superbly sane, superbly balanced in Geneva. It is a careful city. Careful of its heart. It suits me well.

But on the seat by the boats, on the clipped and colourless grass, in the middle of the evening crowds sat this fly-person, weeping.

I passed her, as everybody else was doing, all of us well-dressed as she was, in her hat and fur coat and gloves and beautiful shoes. After I had passed I heard her start to shout and swear, the sobs separated by foul words in a language we none of us quite knew, but all recognised. We all forged ahead, step, step. Two children were walking with a nurse, the little girl hanging back to stare, the boy marching on. The nurse called to her.

"But what is it? What is it, nannie?"

"Oh, come on."

The child watched but, seeing me watching her, turned and ran to the nurse's hand. The bark of the woman's voice knocked about behind us in the trees, and I hurried along the scoured paths, past the dry fountain and the clock which in summer is planted with flowers but today was two metal pointers clamped together against raked earth. She was yelling like Clytemnestra, a hymn of death.

I asked for my key at the hotel foyer and today on duty behind the desk was the head-porter himself, a famous man in

117

Geneva, accustomed to kings. He took his time. I watched the people in the foyer and the lounges, the professional internationals who live with no abiding place, with nothing for every day; whose lives slip off and drop to the ground like a coat as the aeroplane takes off for the next place, who listen with less than half an ear, to messages about the unlikeliness of the aircraft landing on water. Bland and secure. I depend on them for my life.

"Your key, Madame."

I found that I was looking at the key in the magisterial hand. I said, "Not just at present," and left the hotel, crossed the bridge, waited at the time-warp lights, passed the floral clock without flowers and the dead fountain. Only one or two people were left from the short rush-hour, skimpy earwig-people standing watching the choppy lake, the whippy boats. Her bench was now empty.

My father said he didn't call this twelve o'clock. He liked his Sunday dinner at twelve o'clock. He liked *Gardeners' Question Time*.

"I only got back last night, we were working Saturday." (I thought; to anyone else I'd say "on Saturday".)

He said, "Working, you don't know the meaning of working."

In the kitchen he had laid out the usual meat and potatoes and one vegetable – a huge cabbage – flour for the gravy and the pastry, apples to peel for a pie. The oven was not lit. He said, "It'll be tea-time by I get my dinner."

"I've brought the pudding."

"Is it one of them French things?"

"I've been in Geneva, it's a cherry pie."

"Then I'll miss my tart."

He turned the radio up loud so that there was no need to converse. I cooked and tidied after myself – peelings, cabbage stalks – in the threadbare kitchen, opened the back door to see to the dustbins that had to be carried through the house.

His cats slid under my feet. He began methodically, unnecessarily to remove furniture, clear a path for me and the rubbish to pass through to the front-door. I said, "I think I'll do them when I've finished cooking. I don't want to touch food with rubbishy hands." He said, "Good God, it's in bags, isn't it? You know it's your first job, the rubbish," and went back to the fire. "I'm powerless in my own house now."

Flour and fat congealed in the bottom of the meat-tin, slowly thickened, slowly re-liquified as I added cabbage-water. "Bring the wireless in," I yelled. "It's ready."

"I don't like listening and eating," he said, stumbling forward, carrying the radio by its strap on the front of his walking-frame, placing it before him on the table, adjusting the volume upwards. We ate, meat, gravy, cabbage, potatoes to the accompaniment of the instructions about the heating of greenhouses. He said, "It's not a bad pie."

I said, "You don't have a greenhouse."

He said, "Pastry's a bit oily. It's not your mother's pastry."

I said, "Pity you never told her you liked her pastry when she was alive."

He said, "I dare say I'll be getting a greenhouse. Maybe a couple. I've a mind to take up market-gardening."

I wash up. Make him a sponge-cake. Do the rubbish. Wash his clothes. Put them in the drier and it throbs gently. The fire crackles, the 1930s wedding-present clock ticks.

He says, "Driers. Your mother never gave the time of day to one of them things. Hung them all across the yard. Sweet they smelled, like her French childhood."

"It's snowing. Anyway, there's not the time."

"Off again, are you? I've had my ration. Flying off to Monte Carlo. Some people know how to make out. Me all alone. I'm a great age, you know. You'll be sorry when it happens. Never see a soul one week to the next."

"There's hundreds come to see you. All the neighbours."

"Fools. Loads of rubbish."

119

"Meals on wheels."

"Loads of filth."

"I must go now."

"Aye, aye." He sits rocking forwards on the walking-frame, crouched over it, like me in my translator's kiosk. The enclosing bubble is invisible but it's there. Not looking at me he says, "If I sold this house I could go round the world."

"Goodbye, dad."

"Off again. First-class in the morning then, eh?"

"Club-class."

"Might go on a cruise. I'm thinking of it. Goodbye, then." Still not looking at me but vaguely toward the door, sliding a glance he says, "Bye, you're getting fat."

"I'm eight stone."

"Putting on a fair load of weight. All the rich living."

As I close the front-door I say, "I may not be able to come next week." I say it every Sunday, and every Sunday I try not to turn and wave to him from the gate.

All the next week I avoid the Jardin Anglais but on Friday afternoon I am given a ticket for *"Un Spectacle"* which is to be held in the Parc La Grange and can only be reached by walking along the quay. For weeks, posters have been attached to most of the lamp-posts in Geneva advertising this function, and as the arbitration has not risen until five o'clock today, just too late for the evening plane, I accept it. In my room I telephone to change my flight for a Saturday one and find that all are full. So I must stay the week-end. I bath, change, manicure my nails. I had lunch so that I do not need dinner. Nothing to do. There is still an hour before I need leave for the concert and I telephone my father, direct-dial, to tell him that I shan't be home unless I can get a cancellation tomorrow evening. There is no reply. I decide to help myself to gin and tonic from the magic supply. I eat nuts. I ring again. Nothing.

I set off for the *Spectacle*, which is to be held in the Orangerie of the park. In the dark the cold lake splashes.

There is snow about in the Jardin Anglais, triangles of it swept up against the boles of the thin trees. Ice bulges out of the fountain. All the park-benches are empty and I pass the fly's bench carelessly, the singing boats, the gates in the walls of the park, and see the Orangerie shining out across frosted flower-beds.

Inside is the nest all the lamp-post banners flew from: UN SPECTACLE, in bunting, all around the stage. The audience doesn't seem to be very large. It seems in fact to be composed of visitors to Geneva, perhaps all stuck here for the week-end. They have a hangy look and seem to be searching each other's faces to find out why they are here. The great glass-house is boiling hot but glitters cold. The audience is very quiet.

Potted palms. White flowers. A white piano. MOZART HAYDN BRAHMS on white posters. Silence. Coughs. Whispers. A man in evening-dress walks upon the stage. We clap. He holds out a beckoning hand and a woman in evening-dress walks out to join him. He sits at the piano and she prepares to sing. She wears a long black dress and her arm is in a sling. A white sling.

The woman next to me takes off her glasses and looks at me. "A broken arm!" she says, eyebrows high. After the woman has started to sing she turns to me again, and says, "In a sling! She must be German. She could not be Swiss."

As the woman sings – smooth, faultless, bland, douce – I see that she is small and thin, so thin, and her mouth opens in a cave. I get up and make for the door, then out of the glass-house, down the dark paths, through the tropical trees weeping for the sun. The iron gates are locked.

"Who's there?" cried the gate man.

"I want to get out."

"Were you at the *Spectacle*?"

"Yes. I have to get out."

"Sorry, Madame, nobody is allowed to leave the *Spectacle* until the end. The gates are locked until the end of the

Spectacle."

"Is there some other way out?"

He shrugged with a Swiss shrug that has to do only with the neck and jaw.

"Only the wall." He goes back in his box.

Beside the locked gates the wall is low, for the earth for the park has been banked up against it. I step up on it in my Emil Rodin boots, then sit with legs dangling. The other side of the wall drops ten feet and I drop down.

But it is farther than it looks and I have drunk from the fairy-godmother fridge and I feel the heel of my boot break under me. I lie twisted on the grass in my black-silk dress and fur jacket. People passing along through the Jardin Anglais look at me quickly and do not stop. After a time I get up and hop along, slowly, stopping often, holding on to railings, to benches, at one time to the back of the bench on which the fly had sat and wept. In the hotel foyer the concierge sees me and busies himself about his desk. Back in my room I shake, stagger as I try to run a bath, make a grotesquerie of undressing, hobble to the phone to ring my father. There is still no reply so I send for a room-service omelette, turn on the television, watch unseeing. Later I go to bed and my ankle plays a steady tune. Very much later I sleep.

I wake at five-thirty by the lighted digits on the bedside clock and there is another little light, a message-light, beside them; a red dot pulsating from the bedside telephone. Here then it is. It has come.

Dial three for front desk.

"Hello? There is a message for me?"

"Message, Madame?"

"On the telephone. My message-light on the telephone is showing."

"Ah, just one moment, Madame. This is still the night staff."

How long I wait, sitting upright on the bed in the dark. I feel about for the light-switch but it turns on a blast of music.

"Hello – hello? Yes?"

"Yes, Madame, there was a call for you last night. While you were out."

"While I was out – but I was in before ten o'clock."

"I'm sorry, Madame, this is only the night staff. Shall we send it up, Madame?"

"Yes please, at once." My voice is steady. Most commendable.

I take the message as it is flicked under the door. "Shall you be attending the party today? If so I shall call for you, Helmut." (Another translator.)

But I must ring my father, for this is a crossed line. It has some meaning. Party? What party? There is no party that I've heard of. I don't go to parties. I must find the real message.

The phone rings and rings among the tables and chairs, the sideboard, the lithographs, the brass ornaments, the big black group-photographs of my dead mother's dead relations. The hearth-rug is turned back against sparks. Ashes are fallen in the grate. Cold. The tap drips as it has since my childhood. Cats lift their heads, eyes alight at the noise in the dark. Cold. Wind under the front-door. The passage cold, the staircase cold, his bedroom cold and fusty, piled high with his clothes and old boots and old newspapers and gardening magazines. The familiar smell in it of them and of him. In the bed the small hump, the old man gone.

"Hello – what in hell – ?"

"Pa!"

"Who the hell? It's four o'clock in the morning."

"It's me. I'm sorry. It's nearly six here."

"It's four o'clock!"

"Are you all right?"

"What? Yes, I'm all right. I need my shopping doing. Mrs Aylesford's going to do it if she doesn't forget. She's a very funny woman. You have to watch your step with her. I'm in her power of course. If she forgets, I'm finished. Finished. Her and Myrtle. If they've turned funny you'll have to do it

123

tonight, or tomorrow morning at a Sunday-shop. Better get yourself over here this morning. You can stop over the night."

"I'm in Geneva. I've rung because—"

"You're ringing from Geneva? It'll be twenty pound."

"I've hurt my foot."

"You mean you won't be coming?"

I say with assurance and release, "No."

"So who's to get my dinner?"

I have fallen silent.

"Hello? Hello? Well – this is the finish, isn't it? You won't be home the week-end. You won't be home for another week. I'm out of Fairy Liquid."

"Father – where you are is not my home."

"Oh, we know that. No two ways about that. Your mother and I realised that long ago. You made your mother very unhappy."

"I'll see you next week. I rang because I was worried."

"Eh?"

"I thought you were dead. You weren't answering last night."

"No, I wasn't. It was the Euro-Vision Song Contest."

"Goodbye. I've had about enough."

"Oh, I'm sure of that. We're not good enough for you now, your mother and I."

"But mother's dead."

"Eh?"

Helmut is waiting for me in the foyer at twelve o'clock, drinking brandy and staring at the floor. He is a solemn man, a failed barrister, failed everyone thinks because of a profound seriousness that affected the clients. It is said that he insisted on settling every case however clear-cut its impending victory on the grounds that victory in this world is as dust. He is clever, quirkish, can translate into Farsi and, from the gathering gloom on the faces of the unmistakably Iranian delegates in the arbitration in which we are at present engaged, it is possible that his interpretation of some of the admissions carries a whiff of judgment more terrible than this earth can compass. He is a devout Christian and hates travelling on a Sunday, a dear man of enchanting contradictions. At present one hand is knocking back the brandy and the other holding a book of meditations.

We stand waiting for a taxi. Overnight, Geneva has swept up to a peak of cold. A pitiless wind blows the snow and only a few people are about, walking hunched and head down under a white sky. "What is the party, Helmut? I didn't know about a party. Are you sure I'm invited?"

"He said 'all the translators'. I think we're the only two here, though."

"Who is it?"

"The Austrian. The expert-witness. He lives here."

"What does he do when he's not being an expert-witness?"

"Adjusts his monocle. Remembers happier days as interrogator first-class, Sieg Heil, out with the finger-nails. God knows what they all do with themselves, the ex-pat Genevois. Machinate. Fornicate. Play Bridge. The English arbitrator was at church this morning," he added approvingly.

The taxi is taking us out of the city towards the French side of the lake. Near the frontier it veers inland and we are among trees. Large houses stand in clearings, their windows protected by steel mesh. We turn down a narrower road, then a lane, then a gravel drive and at the end of it stands a perfect gingerbread cottage gleaming with fresh paint under the snow, shutters ripple-striped and glossy, window-boxes with heart-shaped rustic cut-outs, burglar-alarms clamped to the eaves. The front door has a peep-hole in it and is surrounded with leaves and berries so highly scarlet they look enamelled. Fabergé. A hen's egg in diamonds. A butler opens the door and from behind him floats the sound of the international Diplomatic élite at play.

We are in the midst. Silk walls, shiny floors, Persian rugs, cherry-wood fires, waitresses with trays of crystal, women in suede as soft as silk and silk as rough as straw. Helmut says, "You'll be all right here, Krista. You will fit like a glove."

"I won't. I'm a wreck. I didn't sleep."

"Always I think, Krista, that you are dressed ready at any time to meet the Queen."

"Ah!" A broad, powdered woman looms in muted tartan. Experienced mouth, experienced eyes. A face that has quelled wars. That has countermanded the launching of a thousand ships.

"We are the translators."

"Ah!" She looks expertly about for the right people for us to meet. It will not be easy. She smiles conspiratorially at Helmut, in a way that means I shall provide for you in a moment, and I am led towards a group where the men are languidly inclining their heads and the women exhaustedly moving their mouths. A man turns to me – vermilion-cheeked, collapsed old mouth, ageing, not well. The woman beside him turns away towards a looking-glass and is gone. A sad smile, mouth turned down at the corners, some hint of a white triangle . . .

"Oh! Was her arm in a sling?"

The red-cheeked man looks puzzled.

"I believe I heard her sing yesterday."

He looks alarmed.

"Oh, I hardly think so. Not many musicians at these do's of ours you know. She's nobody we know. Visitor here. You're English, aren't you? Good guess. Translator at this jamboree at the Metropole?"

"Yes."

"Well – very well paid, isn't it? Jolly good. Like Switzerland, do you?"

"Yes, very—"

"Get a bit of skiing on the side? Jolly good. Know the Mitfords? Not many of them left now. I'm W.H.O. Great place. Air so good. Feel so well. Just married again, how about that? Sixty-six. She's about your age. Heh? Come and meet some people. Here's Sergei."

Glasses are re-filled. Laughter is louder. Sergei looks Slav. Tall. With eye-lids. He holds one arm bent at the elbow across his back. He bows from a great height. He and the vermilion cheeks converse. I am nowhere.

"You are leaving?" the Slav says, surprisingly beside me at the door. "It is soon."

"Yes, I must."

"I too."

He kisses the powdery woman's hand. I thank her but she is looking over my shoulder. At the door we stand for a moment, watching the snow-flakes as his car slides up and his chauffeur approaches with an umbrella. We sink in soft cushions and lie back.

"You are going to a luncheon appointment? Where may I drop you?"

"No. Oh, anywhere near my hotel."

"Certainly not. You shall lunch with me. Have you your passport? Then we shall go to France."

Near Yvoire we leave chauffeur and car beside a bistro at the edge of a village and walk up the middle of an empty street, snow gathering in chunks on the toes of our boots, to the gateway of a château. One great gate leans from a broken hinge. Snow paints its delicate iron roses and plumes. Fastened across the back of the ironwork is old wire-netting and a menu behind a yellowing plastic sheet is tied to it with string. The menu, all but the word MENU, has faded away.

Across the courtyard the door of the château is being opened by the oldest maître d'hotel in the world. He bows. There is a marble and wrought-iron staircase, a black and white marble floor, a desk with a Meissen vase of French graveyard flowers, a dozen clocks – long-case, short-case, ormolu, bell-jar, enamel and gold. Their ticks are water-drops. There is a harp standing outside the dining-room door, two strings gone.

127

And this dining-room must once have been a ballroom. It has long windows looking at the white lake and three tables near them, round, large, all arranged in one corner, thick damask cloths (darned) to the floor. We have a bloomy field of parquet to cross to get to our chairs. The silver forks were forged for Titans, the napkins, small counterpanes dimly patterned with lilies. There are no other diners, no sound of life, no smell of food but a tiled stove with little eighteenth-century scenes of Vaud reaches the ceiling and the great room is alive from it, pleasant and warm. Pad, pad across the parquet comes the ancient with wine upon a tray. We talk of Sergei's childhood home in old Bohemia.

And then the caviar. And then the borsch. And then woodcock. And then a camembert. And then a cream pudding. And then a glass of candied fruits that shine in the snowy light. And then coffee and a bilberry liqueur.

And then, I supposed, bed.

But this is my misfortune. I do not now like bed.

I go to find a cloak-room. I sit at a dressing-table with silver brushes, look at my face in a glass so old that it is exploding with bronzy stars. A flattering, greeny light. This is a brothel for international moguls, for giants, for great white whales (I am woozy with wine) and I am a minnow, a sprat, a wafer of plankton to float almost invisible through their jaws.

Not that he looks like a whale. He looks a gentle man.

He is waiting for me on a sofa in the hall and there is nobody else anywhere to be seen. He gets up, takes my elbow, draws me down beside him. He says, "I believe that the answer will be no."

I say, "I'm afraid so," through a wave of disappointment. And memory.

"Let's sit here a moment until the car comes. Where may I take you home?"

We sit on in silence. He is looking at me all the time and says that I am beautiful. "Beautiful," he says. "But so frightened. I understand it," and he stretches out his left

128

hand. "You must look."

"I – yes, I noticed."

"You didn't like seeing me eat."

"I – no. I don't mind—"

"Some women of course like it. It thrills them. Hold my hand."

I stretched out and took the gloved hand and under the leather it is hard and wooden. Hard and dead.

"It is the result of Stalingrad."

"It's wonderful," I said. "How could it be made?"

"It's an old miracle now. A German miracle. Before its time, like Ming china."

I close my eyes and try to think of things that are living and complete. Un-secretive and open. My father's face keeps getting in the way. I stroke the hand and he says, "You are thinking of the contraption at the wrist when I take it off. And what happens at night."

"I was thinking nothing of the sort," I say and hold the glove all the way back to the hotel. As he kisses my living hand on the steps of the hotel he says, "I believe you to have been very unhappily married." Then he kisses my cheek and the snow-flakes swim past us, large and light and lacy in front of the glitzy revolving doors.

There are four carrots in a row, nose to tail. Six potatoes. Four rashers of bacon and a gigantic chicken on a plate. Nearby stands a jelly-square upon a saucer. The old linoleum on the kitchen floor, the cupboard tops, sink, look as if they have been scrubbed daily for several hours. Cats sit outside on the sill with frantic dinner-time eyes. I unpack the food I have brought, light the gas.

"You may as well know—" he calls through.

"Yes?"

No reply.

I go back to the sitting-room. He doesn't move. "Did you see the chocolates I brought you?"

"You may as well know—"

"What?"

"I'm getting married."

"Oh yes. Who to?"

"Mrs Aylesford."

There is a tapping at the back door. It is Mrs Aylesford with pots of marmalade. "How d'you find him?" She leans forward, bright-eyed.

"He says you're going to be married, Mrs Aylesford."

"Me? Whoever to?"

"To him."

"Yes. He's getting worse. I've brought you some marmalade. He ought to be cared for, Krista."

"But he's perfectly all right. He's very well."

"Not if he thinks he's getting married to me."

"But he doesn't. Not really. He has to say things like that. It's boredom – boredom. Look how he's arranged all those carrots."

We survey the line of carrots.

"Last week," I say, "he was thinking of going on a cruise. Oh, I do wish he would go on a cruise."

"You ought to take him off foreign with you," she watches me. Interested. Examines my clothes. "Eh. Krista?"

He appears in the kitchen doorway and seeing Mrs Aylesford says, "Oh, God," and shuffles off again.

"Can't even keep away when I've got my daughter here," he says. "My only daughter. My only child. It's a pity you weren't a boy. Where's my dinner?"

"If I was a boy you wouldn't have me cooking your dinner. You wouldn't get a son doing what—"

"And what's this about me going off foreign? I can't do with foreign stuff," he says, scooping away at Mövenpick Black Forest cake.

"She says I should take you with me abroad."

"The trouble with this world is," he says, taking more cream, "the way people can't be satisfied with being in one place. If people all kept to their own homes—"

"If they kept to their own homes you'd never have met mother."

"Well. That was a mistake. My marriage to your mother. All these foreign languages. Foreign tongues. Everything better somewhere else – that's it, isn't it? Grass in the next field. Going off to these chocolate-box places."

He examines the chocolates I've brought, prodding them for the soft ones. "They can't even print a key to these things now. They used to put a card in."

"Switzerland isn't really chocolate-box."

"It's picture-postcard."

"It's full of – full of pain. Like everywhere."

"Now I've got a bloody brazil."

"I went out with a man last week who'd had a hand burned off. At Stalingrad."

"Now Stalingrad. That was a very terrible thing. Month after month. How old was the bugger? Must have been my age."

When I have carried out the rubbish he says, "Full of pain, is it? Switzerland? I went there once. Faces like emery-boards. Hard-mouthed Nazis. You're over-sensitive, that's your trouble. You're like me."

I sit down behind him and cover my face with my hands. I hang on to one good thing – that he cannot mention my marriage.

After a time he says, "Where've you gone? What you sitting behind me for? I'm in everybody's clutches."

On my way to work on Monday I saw the fly again. We met head on, on a corner of the Rue Versonnex outside the shop with the glassy pillars. I side-stepped a moment, avoiding somebody and suddenly there she was, loping forward towards me with her black lost eyes. She was not this time crying but there was all the frenzy there, lashed down but as fierce as at the first encounter. She looked hard at me and passed.

Under my bubble the words flow out. We are on one of the last few witnesses now. This one drones on and on about the wrongs and rights of a machine-tool being employed to dig a dam in Baghdad. "As we have stated before" – endless parentheses – "As we have stated before, in a way quite incontrovertible, whereas the statements submitted on Day Sixteen by Mr Bronx concerning point number two hundred and forty-seven on the question of costs of the extra-hyper – digger equipment and in conjunction with Mr Jinx's evidence concerning point number three hundred and eighty-six, of statement number nine hundred and five on Day Thirty-Six, I will submit that, notwithstanding . . ."

The words pour from him. The words pour from me, from Helmut, from the other two. The clock on the wall with its twelve dots, its stubby fingers, never seems to move.

Towards the end of the week Helmut is waiting by the door for me at lunch time. "You all right? Like some lunch?" We go over towards the Old Town and passing along the Verson-nex, towards the shop with the glittering pillars, suddenly two great lymphatic people appear holding the hands of a retarded child, and I reach out and grab Helmut's sleeve.

He looks surprised. Nobody touches Helmut. As we go through the Place des Eaux Vives he looks at me again and draws quite close to me. "You don't often see those in Geneva. They keep them off the streets. What is it?" He takes my arm and we go up over the cobblestones to a restaurant under the arches, warm and dark, red and white table-cloths, Italian, almost empty. As we wait, Helmut takes out a Missal. When the spaghetti comes he puts the book carefully away in his pocket and says, "You are beginning to look a little better."

"I'm all right. Why?"

"You look so ill. Is it money, sex or sickness?"

"It's none of them. I have no reason – It's just that there's so much damage. So much pain."

"Geneva? Damage? Pain?"

"Yes. All kept under wraps. Everywhere in the world."

He pauses with a forkful of carbonara and says, "But it's you who keep yourself under wraps."

"I don't know how not to. But it's not just fancy. Haven't you noticed here? It's a crime to be miserable in public. It is indecent. Indecent to be open."

He says, "You know, I think it is this most bloody of all arbitrations. You need a rest. But I like Geneva."

"I'm frightened, Helmut."

"Of what?"

"I keep seeing this woman. She's like a fly."

He regards me, courteously.

After the hearing that day I saw Helmut talking to the English arbitrator who came over to me as I left my kiosk. "Bear up," he said, "not much longer."

"This week?"

"Oh, definitely this week. Maybe even tomorrow. Come for a drink."

We walked, the elderly man and I, down to the lake-side restaurant on the Rue du Rhône, full of the very young – silky hair, pale suits, Pathek Philippe watches. Among them the English arbitrator looked comfortable, shabby and wise. We sat silent, listening to all the talk about money and he said, "Sorry. I thought it might be more interesting. Young and gay for you. Why do you keep looking over your shoulder?"

"Oh – I just thought – I thought I saw someone."

"Aha, you are being followed. You are a spy. Something to do with Swedish Sergei of the wooden claw."

"I didn't know he was Swedish. He said he was at Stalingrad. I only had lunch with him."

"I'm sure. He's homosexual. But charming. You were very safe. Did you know that the police in Geneva have a file on every foreigner working here? There's one about me and there will be one about you."

"There's absolutely nothing they could find to say about me. Oh!—"

The fly was there. Standing outside, looking in at me through the glass.

"Sweet child," he said. "What is it? You look nearly out of your wits. Come on – you're not being followed, you know. Drink your drink. Bear up. We really are almost finished now, and when it's over I am going to give us all a huge and wonderful party at the Perle du Lac."

On the Friday – for of course the case lasted out the week: it was to resume for a final day on Monday – he came across again as I dashed for the plane and said, "Helmut's going home with you. Right to your front-door."

And on my front doorstep – Helmut a little disorganised by three Bloody Marys and St John of the Cross on the plane – I said, "What do you think is wrong with me?" And he said, "I think you know."

"But I don't. What?"

He said. "I don't. You do. Somewhere."

I said to him, "Listen, there is a woman like a fly. I see her everywhere. I saw her this week looking through a window at me at the Rue du Rhône and if you want to know I saw her just now in the luggage hall going through the Goods to Declare. It's the first time she has followed me home."

"I think you will understand in time."

"She has little hands and they were clutching the handle of the trolley and her mouth was a cave."

He said, "Krista, all will be well."

My car wouldn't start the next morning and I had to take the tube to South Wimbledon and walk over to my father's. It is a mile from the station so that it was half-past ten by the time I reached his gate and saw the curtains all drawn across the windows and a notice pinned to his front door.

The pulsating bedside light.

134

It was a typed message inside a transparent plastic bag with a drawing-pin at each corner, neat and straight. "Dear Krista," the message read, "please call immediately next door, number 38, and oblige E. Aylesford." I took out my key and went immediately upstairs to my father's bedroom.

The cats shot out as I opened the door and found him under his old satin eiderdown. He was staring at the ceiling like an effigy.

"Pa – are you ill?"

No reply. I went to the bedside and sat down and wished that I could bear to hold his hand. He had humped himself over now with his head in the corner, his knees drawn up. He began to cry.

"What is it? Pa? She said I had to go in next door first—"

At once he was sitting upright in the bed, hair on end, eyes staring.

"She, what? Who?"

"Mrs Aylesford."

"Where is she?"

"I don't know. She put a message on the door."

"Which door?"

"The front-door."

"My front-door? With glue?"

"With drawing-pins."

"She stuck drawing-pins in my front-door? I'll kill that woman. She's not right in her mind. Where were you last night? What about the shopping?"

"Why are you lying in bed in the dark?"

He collapsed again and began to whimper into the eiderdown.

"It's because it's all a myth."

"What is?"

"Heaven."

"I'd better go and see Mrs Aylesford."

"Leave her alone. It's a myth, isn't it?"

"I don't know."

135

"They all go on. Churches. Parsons. There's never anyone to prove it. Nobody's ever come back. Heaven! When you die you're dead. Look at your mother."

"I don't know."

"They're all gone, aren't they? All the old ones. Everyone. You stop, that's what you do. Go out. And all the things you've missed. Look at what you missed with Graham."

And so – he had said it.

I left him and went up Mrs Aylesford's path and saw her through her front-room window, waiting for me. Myrtle from number 32 was sitting with her and they were talking simultaneously, nodding their heads up and down. "Come in, Krista, we've been waiting for you such a time. Would you like a cup of tea?"

It was all laid out ready, with tea-spoons and sugar-lumps and a lace tray-cloth. As Mrs Aylesford went out for the tea-pot Myrtle lit a cigarette and said, "Cold, isn't it? No sign of spring yet."

"Is it something important, Mrs Aylesford?"

She was fussing with the hot-water jug. "Biscuits, Krista? They're Nice biscuits. Or talking to you I suppose I should say Neece biscuits. It's funny, you never know how to say it. They always seem so English somehow."

"Is it about Father, Mrs Aylesford?"

She was busy with a tea-strainer. Then she put a little plate with a biscuit on it by my cup. Then she settled carefully in her chair. "Well, yes, dear, it is. I'm afraid the time has come for me and Myrtle to speak out. And others agree, down the terrace."

"You're worried?"

"Oh, very worried. Aren't we, Myrtle."

"We're distracted sometimes. Distracted."

"I know," I said, "you've been most terribly good and kind. I know he's very difficult—"

"Oh, it's not that he's difficult. We're quite used to difficult people, aren't we, Myrtle? There's been half a dozen in the terrace difficult but we haven't minded. There was poor Mrs Cross who left me her china, she used to have to sleep sitting up. Well, she died sitting up and I couldn't get her flat. Her back broke right through. She was worn away to cornflakes, wasn't she, Myrtle?"

"Cornflakes. Her bones were cornflakes."

"And we had a terrible time with next door the other side, he used to sleep by day and work by night. Do-it-yourself, and all those dogs. I daren't tell you the state the house was in when he went. Well, we were the ones that found him. It hadn't happened long. The social services commended us. They said we must have suffered, living so near. It took a fortnight to get the place clean and the bottles out."

"How good you are. But you don't have any of that with Father?"

"Oh no. Nothing like that." They looked in their tea-cups, spinning it out. The long-planned encounter.

"Well, Krista, it's his rudeness. It's his cruelness."

"Oh, he can be cruel," said Myrtle.

"It's the things he says. The terrible cruel things."

"And he's a bit sexy too. I don't like telling you this and you his daughter and him so old. You'd think he'd have forgotten. I suppose it must be a sub-conscious thing like Freud. And he's so miserable. And so horrible."

"I know," I said, "that he's a great pessimist."

"Pessimist, Krista, he's in black despair. And it's not right because he passes it on. All about no heaven and this life being hell, and all about death."

"He never leaves death alone," said Myrtle. "Never. He keeps appearing in that door. Standing there with his eyes blazing. Here, in Mrs Aylesford's front doorway saying, 'Where will it end? I'll tell you where – it'll end here and now and forever' – doesn't he, Mrs Aylesford? 'Here and now. Cancer or a stroke. Or an overdose or slit-my-wrists.' It's terrible."

"It's like a bad angel. We can't take any more of it, Krista.

137

And then last night – well, that's when we knew we had to speak to you."

"I'm so sorry. I couldn't get over last night."

"Oh, I'm sure you're very busy. You have a very busy life with all your foreign travel. Mr Aylesford and I always found holidays abroad very tiring."

"What happened?"

"Well, he wandered off. I'm afraid, Krista, he wandered off and we had to call the police. That's why he's in bed today. He had quite a long session at the police-station – talking about sins and you and rubbish. He had to see a police doctor."

"I've been up to see him. He doesn't seem very ill."

Their four eyes were excited and hostile. " 'Physically,' the police doctor said, 'physically, he's wonderful'."

"It's mentally," said Myrtle, "it's mental trouble. He went on and on to the policeman about his shame."

"What shame?"

"Oh, I'm sure I don't know. I expect it's something private to the family." They looked uneasy. "But altogether – I'm afraid we had to report to the police that in our opinion – and of course we're not professionals; this is simply the opinion of the terrace – we think he ought to be Assessed. In a home. He's a damaged man."

"In an asylum," said Myrtle. "Or any rate a Nerve Home."

"Yes," said Mrs Aylesford, "I mean especially, Krista, if he's going to start walking away. He went all the way to Wimbledon Park pond and started going for all the lads with their remote controls for being so noisy. He said something very disgusting to them which I'll not repeat."

There was a welcome, though unhealthy silence.

I said, "I'll go and talk to him for a bit. I'm so sorry."

"I think we'll have to have something a bit more definite than that, Krista."

"Yes, of course. The job I'm doing comes to an end on

Monday. I can be here perhaps by Monday night. I'll speak to the doctor. If you could just hold the fort till then—"

"You didn't ever think, Krista, of having him up to live with you?"

"Yes. I did. I have asked him. He has always said no."

"I expect he's just not wanting to be troublesome."

"Well, that isn't exactly usual. And he does realise I work abroad most of the time."

"Oh, yes."

"But I think," said Mrs Aylesford, "that we all have to make sacrifices for our parents, don't you? I mean money's not everything and it's in the Bible."

"But I have to work, Mrs Aylesford."

"Yes, it's hard when you're not married. But with the money you could get for his house. Or for your house – ? Another biscuit? It would break our hearts here to see him in a Nerve Home."

The bed was empty when I went back next door but I could see him dressed and out in the back-garden on his walking-frame lunging about at a large tree with the pruning-shears. I said, "The dinner's warming up in the oven. You'll get cold out there. Come back in."

"I've never had a cold in my life. Mind, I'm breaking up otherwise."

"You look very well. I hear you took yourself off for a walk?"

"I've got five black toes."

"Have you shown the doctor?"

"I know what he'd say. And I know what he'd think, too. Corruption – that's what it is. Decay. I'm decaying. I'm getting started in good time. For my box."

"Pa – will you promise not to go off on your own again. You're frightening next door."

"They need frightening. They need something to get them out of bed in the morning. All they do is sit and yatter. My

139

going off's the biggest thing that's ever happened to them. Gives them orgasms."

"They think you should come and live with me."

"I wouldn't live with you," he said, "if it was the atomic bomb."

But, as I finished washing up and hanging up the tea-towels and putting on my coat, he was crying by the fire. "You never liked me," he said. "And I never liked you."

I said, "Oh, Pa. I'll be back on Tuesday at the latest. I'll come over and stay with you. I'll take some time off."

"A lot of use you'll be. What use is anyone? What's it all mean? You can't tell me. And I wouldn't come near that fancy place in Putney bought with Graham's money, not if you prostrated yourself in the road."

"I'm going then."

"Where? Now? Leaving me all alone? You're not going off tonight in that aeroplane? Not after all that's happened."

Usually I call him before I leave for Heathrow but tonight, as I stood looking at the telephone, asking for strength, it began to ring and at the same moment the door-bell started ringing, too. I thought, "Taxi – I'll get it first," and found instead Helmut on the step muffled up and holding his usual plastic carrier full no doubt as usual with prayer-books, whisky, tooth-brush, electric razor, two shirts. No one ever calls for me.

"I must just get the phone."

"I've come to pick you up. The taxi's waiting."

Not quite asking him in I said, "Oh yes. Right. Hang on," picked up the receiver and heard Mrs Aylesford's voice. I was surprised that after the great pleasure I had just felt on seeing Helmut I could be swept into equal distress that it was not my father.

And there seemed to be something else. Something over my shoulder, some shadow, something black and bad that was considering me carefully. "Yes, Mrs Aylesford?"

"I'm very sorry to have to say, Krista, I'm very sorry to be the bearer of bad news, but he's gone again."

"But I'm just leaving to catch my plane."

"I'm sure I'm very sorry but—"

"I have to catch it. I can't let them down. It is the last day, tomorrow. There is nobody else to do my work. He can't be far."

"It is a very dark night, Krista."

"Oh, Lord. I'll ring the police. How long—"

"I saw him about twenty minutes ago. I took him his tea. He was crying, Krista. I'm afraid he was saying you had been very unkind—"

"Yes, I see. All right."

"I can't go," I said to Helmut. "My father's disappeared."

He took the phone.

"This is a friend of Krista. Please explain to me the situation."

There was an interested pause. Then I heard her voice, hesitant, then more confident, then furiously clacking.

"We shall telephone you from the airport if there is time, otherwise from Geneva. In the meantime, kindly get in touch with the police. Krista will be back as soon as possible. Goodnight."

Clack, clack, squawk.

"Good evening."

Half-way to Heathrow I said, "I can't possibly go, you know."

"The woman Aylesford said that he does this often."

"She has never told me that." I looked. Short-legged, tight-lipped, fierce-nosed Sir Thomas More. Archetypal immovable lawyer. He said, "I pressed her."

"But I can't go. Not knowing."

Walking behind me in the cafeteria queue (the plane had been delayed an hour) he said, "I think that we should now sit down and that you should talk to me. I am right in thinking that you are in some way obsessed with your father and he

141

with you?"

"No, of course not. What's the matter with me is that I am going mad. I keep seeing – oh, God! I told you. You didn't take any—"

"You told me that you keep seeing a woman who looks like a fly. The name of the fly I suggest to you – " he looked at the postage-stamp-sized packet of biscuits on my tray and added a doughnut, "The name of this fly is Guilt."

Eating the doughnut, or rather picking it up and putting it down again, I said, "I dare say."

"Are we, I wonder, in the areas of child-abuse, incest or cruelty?"

"Of course not."

"Why of course not?"

"Not in the terrace."

"My dear, you little know. Why do you feel guilty about your father?"

"I don't know. I told him something once I shouldn't have done. I said I was sorry. It was just once. I have done all I can for him. I suppose not enough. I suppose I ought to love him more – or show something more. But there seems no more that I can possibly do."

"You feel pity?"

"Oh yes, I do feel pity. You see he is so sane. His trouble is not senility or insanity but a most rare sanity. He really does look steadily at the nature of death and is terrified. He talks about it. What he says is all true. Other people can't face it. He sounds so dotty but he says what's really in all our hearts."

"There is no need for him however to have destroyed your happy young spirit."

"I'm not sure I had one."

"Yes, you did. We all did. Sometimes deeply secreted. He has been murderous. Why has he?"

"I don't know."

"Perhaps," Helmut said, "the woman you see, the fly, is not your guilt but his? Is there something he may feel guilty about?"

"Plenty that he should—"

"But is there?"

And so I told it.

"It was my husband. He was thrilled by him. He fawned over him. By my marrying important Graham he had bolstered himself. He strutted. He used to say, 'They'll think a bit more of me now.' As if it had been my duty to do it for him."

"Did Graham like him?"

"He loathed him. He couldn't bear to be in the same room with him. He didn't see that he was sad or frightened and he never found him funny. He made excuse after excuse not to see him. In the end he said if I couldn't free myself from my father he was going. And in the end he went."

"Did your father know the reason for his going?"

"I told him. I told him once. I broke open. I screamed it at him. Afterwards I couldn't believe I'd done it. Since then he has been much worse to me."

"Yes, of course he has. Your father is wanting you to leave him. To withdraw from him. Chuck him."

"Leave him? He rules me. He devours me. He weeps to keep me."

"He wants you to leave him alone. If he can see you free and happy, then his guilt about your marriage will go away."

"You're saying he loves me?"

"Yes. But let me tell you, Krista, if you do not do something decisive, when he dies the fly, Guilt, will spawn a disgusting maggot called Remorse who will be with you always."

"Since you've never met him—"

"It is not necessary. I know you."

The plane was signalled. I said, "You mean I must not go home tonight?"

"Your home is not with him."

"Helmut, he is out-of-doors, alone, lost in the dark. He is

143

very old. Can't you think what they'll all say?"

"For the love of God, forget what they'll all say. If ruthlessly, selfishly, wordlessly you do not leave for Geneva now, tonight, you will be damaged forever, destroyed, and he will die a guilty and unhappy man. You have to set him free. Get your passport."

On the plane he said, "All right?" but I didn't answer.

At the hotel he said, "And now I am coming with you to your room." The concierge's hand paused over the keys. "From which we shall telephone together." At my bedroom door he said, "And be prepared for anything."

"You mean – the fly?"

"Fuck, Krista, the fly. I mean – ah yes."

The message-light was on. Helmut picked up the phone, dialled downstairs, spoke to the operator. Then said, "Your father has telephoned you."

"He has telephoned *me*? Here? Telephoned Geneva?"

"Now I shall ring the neighbour Aylesford."

I sat on a chair by the bathroom door and listened, as he listened, undoing his long scarf, removing his gloves, hat, then his coat with all the time the receiver under his chin. Then he put down the phone and said, "Your father is safe home. He is in bed." He went to examine the fridge, came back to the bed, sat on it and began to unpeel one of my good-night chocolates.

"You can't stay here," I said, "I'm not having it said that all I needed was a man."

"All you needed was an ally," he said, removing his shoes, "An expert witness. But please, you must pull yourself up, Krista. You are looking most wild and untidy and your mouth is a hole."

We lay side by side on the bed and I said, "I must ring him back."

He said, "In a minute," and took hold of my wrist.

"I love him," I said.

"Wait ten minutes."

When it was half an hour he said, "Ring later." And then it was much later, and too late, and then it was morning and only half an hour to get to the arbitration.

In the taxi we sat hand in hand, and the lake flying past, the throb of the terrible packed traffic on the bridge – the fact of not having telephoned was the faintest shadow. At twelve o'clock the last, the incredible, scarcely believed-in last session ended without histrionics or perorations, a simple unremarkable end to the years and years of patient argument in Teheran and Rome and here. It ended with a nodding, a relaxation between the parties, a smiling and sitting back among the arbitrators and the pause before the great pack-up of papers for shipment home about the world. The court began to chatter in its different languages, drawing away into groups. Babel once more.

"And the faces of the translators are suffused with joy," said the English arbitrator to Helmut and me, as we stood together, "See you in half an hour at the Perle du Lac."

"Oh, I can't. I must get home. There's a bit of a crisis—"

"Couldn't you ring from the restaurant?"

"You would have heard if there were anything," said Helmut.

But at the Perle, with its glass walls against the lake and sudden sunlight on the mountains and the snows, I forgot. We celebrated until the four o'clock plane. Champagne and rosy table-cloths and flowers and Helmut touching my fingers.

The house was all in darkness, but next door Mrs Aylesford's lights were on. I was alone and walked to her window. She and Myrtle were seated facing the blank television screen, their backs solid, rather stooped. Myrtle was smoking and staring at the floor. Mrs Aylesford had knitting idle on her lap. On the sofa facing the window and looking straight at me, sat the fly.

AFTER THE
STRAWBERRY TEA

WHEN the last removal van had groaned away up the blos-
somy street she was alone in the hall of the empty house in the
April night.

Her husband was still upstairs, thumping from room to
room, opening and shutting doors, checking catches on
windows. "Don't go in to the spare-room," she called, "Not
for a moment. The cat's there. Leave him till last."

He did not answer. She heard him closing each door,
slowly, carefully, in preparation for setting the burglar-alarm.
The bathroom door was a loose one. Three out of four times it
sprang open, and set the siren going. It had to be coaxed.
How long would it take the new people to learn that? Ought
she to leave a note?

In the middle of the silky parquet of the hall stood a bottle
of champagne with a ribbon round it: their present to the new
people when they walked in tomorrow morning with their
babies and Philippino nannies, as she and James had walked
in thirty years ago with babies only, little money and a quarter
of a van-load of belongings; James with his wild red hair,
laughing and calling out at the wonderful space. He had been
between jobs then, with a huge mortgage and drunk with
optimism. Elisabeth looked at the champagne bottle which
swelled before her eyes as tears came. "Oh, come," she said,
"For goodness sake," and took a clean handkerchief and
held it hard against the space between her top lip and her
nose. For the move she was wearing a grey wool suit. She had
planned to do so, to leave properly dressed, her image in
order. Over the years she had had many images. Now, at sixty
and very composed, she liked to think that she had an

experienced face, rather after the nature of Dame Peggy Ashcroft's, though of course younger. She could call up this image with a flick, like taking out a powder-compact. She could tune in at any time to what her friends often said, "D'you know who Elisabeth reminds me of? Peggy Ashcroft." It was a complex triumph, something won.

Thirty years ago she had not looked like Peggy Ashcroft. When she had had time to consider it she had thought that she would like to look like Audrey Hepburn but knew that this was beyond desire, except for the skin and bone. She had not looked like anyone much in those days and certainly not like herself (one never does that) for she had not come together as a person. Oh, the terrible photograph with the three babies under the pear-tree – her hollow eyes, her Belsen bones, right-angled hips sticking out through the lampshade fifties dress. Worn-out, she'd looked, and had been worn out, never facing that she was non-domestic, non-maternal, needing a job. Always she had tried too hard – wasting time painting pictures of herself that were right for the landscape, the house and rich South-London suburb. The waste of desire – that the children should all be in the right clothes, go to the right schools, do the right things: dancing-class, piano lessons, recorder lessons, Sunday School at St Mary's, extra Latin.

Oh, those right schools. How she had suffered. The O Levels, the A Levels, the University entrances, the anguish in case they didn't get first-class honours. All the things she in her heart least cared about.

And oh, the childhood illnesses – all the time the illnesses, each one seeming her own personal failure, each time thinking, well, I'll be able to cope with the next, and finding in the next the same seeds of dread. The long looks given her by down-to-earth cleaning-ladies who could crash round three houses in the road before four o'clock and zip back down to Raynes Park in their smart cars to crash about in their own house and cook for a family.

The floating population of the old house these past thirty

148

years. The dailies and the au pairs. The short horror of the mad nannie, who had turned up for the last child. The French nurse-maid who had come next and felt always cold and lonely and had stood outside doors, creaking on the floor-boards, listening, and who had fallen in love with James, though by then his head had been bald and his walk grave. Her adoration had made him graver still – but, thought Elisabeth, very delighted.

And oh, the Strawberry Teas and little fork-suppers they had given in the garden for the NSPCC. And the enormous children's parties, and the Guy Fawkes celebrations which were always so frightening and you couldn't enjoy until they were over and the last child gone un-incinerated home. Yet how we missed them later when the fireworks were banned.

And all the Christmases. The hanging-up of Christmas cards about the hall on strings and the way they all blew down. Other people's cards had always stayed firmly in place, solid rows fixed together with a stapler; just as other people's Christmas trees had always stood up straight and didn't drop half an inch of needles. Ours was always huge and queer, she thought, bought at the last minute with the angel crammed in at the top pressed against the ceiling, as if she had a head-ache. James had always been too busy to see to – or even to see – these things.

And the road. This road. Not usual. All of us in each other's pockets. All moving out here at about the same time, years and years ago when the Rent Act kicked us out of London. How well we all know each other, she thought. Scarcely anybody has ever moved away.

Oh, the births and the deaths and the marriages. The runnings-away of wives or husbands, and the runnings-back. The careful babyhoods becoming children's technicolour adolescences, dwindling usually into very tolerable sort of marriages. Oh, the secrets we all know about each other she thought. The extended, non-nuclear, intricate, beautiful sub-urban family.

The telephone calls up and down this road these thirty years, she thought. First they had been to do with the co-operative at the school gate, later the fetchings and carryings to parties, later still the terrors of the small hours when fetchings and carryings were no longer possible. "Is Emily with you? No, not yet. No, she said with you." "I'll come round." "Oh, thanks. Oh no – no, it's all right. I think I can hear her feet on the gravel. I'll kill her."

And love, she thought. The stirrings of love all these years in the people of the road. The frissons, the well-behaved romances. The not so well-behaved romances. The not-exactly-affaires. The affaires. The roaring emotional bon-fires. The sad retreats indoors. And the highs and lows of husbands – their office lives, their silences. Husbands coming up the hill from the station at night, each with his heavy briefcase, grey-faced from the city.

And not only husbands. Even thirty years ago most wives in the road had worked and were to be seen trudging up the hill too, in young London clothes, case in one hand, expensive bag of frozen supper in the other.

Not Elisabeth. Exhausted by her private premonition of failure Elisabeth had gone plugging on, doing what she was not good at – though the children flourished and never went off the rails, James didn't leave her and her frail romances never really threatened – Elisabeth continuing all day at home, striving and drudging and adoring. Her adoration (if that's what it really was, she thought) of the children had filled her life so deeply that they had grown sick of her and fled. But she had continued to think of them most of the time (James now often abroad) as she toiled in her garden, and spent a fortune (James had grown rich) on idiot beautification of the house.

Never beautification of herself though. She had thought, in the first years, when money was uncertain and private school-fees high and James's expenses in the city phenomenal, that she could always save on clothes. James never noticed what she wore, nor did the children. One of the au pairs had said – the Parisian with the Gucci jeans – that she looked her best in gardening clothes, and this had pleased her. Countrified. Unsuburban. Someone with peasant strength, she thought. Non-competitive.

That all seemed so long ago. She had begun to change, to think, to resent, when the last child had left home and the romantic monster of a Victorian house had fallen silent.

" 'When the last King,' " said Elisabeth, " 'Has gone in to the dark' ".

James gave a final slam to the playroom door whose little battered brass knob had a rattly sound. The playroom had been the maids' room a hundred years ago. Outside it a jangly bell on a wire disappeared through the floor to a housekeeper's room somewhere below. When the bell had jangled three maids had rolled out of bed to wash their faces with cold water in a tin bowl, grumbling in the dawn. Often an icy dawn. No heating then.

No maids now. Elisabeth had been maid, cook, housekeeper, chatelaine, nurse, governess, social-secretary, mistress, mother, wife. And creator, she thought, looking round her now in these last minutes. Though the house had grown emptier it had not died and would not yet. Some of her would stay in it. Perhaps this host of women who were herself hadn't done too badly.

They were leaving behind their carpets and curtains and light-fittings. The drawing-room was open. She had never had much furniture in the drawing-room and from here it looked just the same. Unthinkable that if she were to step in now there would not be all the books on the shelves, and the long yellow watered-silk sofa, which had once been the long corduroy sofa with three legs and a dark patch at one end where for years children had rested their heads watching a television-set now banished to a bedroom; and another dark dent at its far end, where their feet had rested. "Take off your *shoes*," Elisabeth's voice had cried over two decades. The great fledgling children had lain on mesmerised, feeling about like blind people for scattered Coke-cans, and apples.

Illnesses and doctors' dread messages, betrothals and pregnancies had been announced in that room; and, when she had one day picked up the telephone, her mother's death. A daughter had suddenly come back to them there, stepping in from the garden carrying the neat overnight bag she had once used for dancing class. It had been after the girl's first holiday alone with a man. Far too soon. Her daughter had looked aggressive, rebellious, deeply tired, and a child again. "Did you have a nice time darling?" The shy question, shy and miserable.

"Awful thanks." The shy and miserable answer.

James came down the staircase carrying the cat in its basket. He'd pushed it in back to front. There was only the hump of its astounded back visible through the wires and an electrified-looking tail. "All done," said James, "Right. I'll do the alarm. Keys?"

"I have them."

"We'll slam and then drop them back through the letterbox. They have their own for tomorrow. All right?"

"Yes." (Handkerchief still pressed.)

"Right then. Coming? Sweetheart?"

She nodded. Pressing hard. James stood, hesitating between bluster and grief. The hall echoed, swam huge. The cat-basket swung in his hand. His feet, crossing to the door were loud on the wood. Elisabeth stood still.

"We must go," he said, and stopped, looking out of the window, "It's fearfully late. Nearly midnight. We said we'd be gone by five."

"The packers," she said, "So slow. We said we'd have dinner when we got there. At The Bell."

"Are you hungry?"

"No, not a bit. Are you?"

"No. We'll have breakfast at The Bell instead. Come on Liz. It's a two-hour drive. Who's that?"

Beside the garden gate in the shadowy night stood a woman.

"There's someone out there. Whoever is it?"

The woman turned a little and looked up, then down the road and then up at the sky. Her face caught the light from the porch – a lean pale face.

"It's that dotty woman. That crazy woman."

"Who?" Elizabeth walked across and looked out of the window, too. "It's Mrs Apse," she said. "Poor old Hilary Apse."

"But it's midnight. She's about ninety. What's she doing out at midnight? I hope to hell she's not come to say goodbye."

"We hardly know her."

"You didn't ask her to the farewell-party."

"Well, of course not. She's so old. I thought she never went out. I thought she was in a Home. I haven't seen her for years."

"She used to come to the Strawberry Tea."

"So did everyone – all her friends. They're nearly all dead, all those old ones are. They were our age when we moved here. She used to walk her dog at night. You used to see her lingering about at night in the streets. With the dog. Years ago."

"It's what she must be doing now."

"She always looked as if she'd had an interesting life somewhere."

"She's still having it," said James. "She's far from home. The Grange is twenty minutes away. I'll go and have a word."

"I can't go off with her watching," said Elisabeth. "I'm sorry, I can't. It's private. We've had the farewell party. They've all had the sense to leave us alone tonight. I'm not going out while she's there."

"I'll see to it."

James left the house, walking fast down the path, and Elisabeth heard the car-door open and slam as the cat was settled in, wire mesh to the back so that the motorway lights wouldn't upset him. She heard James's voice and a high, light antique sound that was Mrs Apse's voice. Soon she saw James walking with Mrs Apse along the road to the corner of the garden fence. They turned together, walking slowly, James's head politely inclined, and disappeared into the narrow snicket that connected with the parallel quiet street. When James returned he found the last lights of the old house out, the front door closed, the garden-gate tight shut as it never was, and Elisabeth in the car, eyes front, hands folded, and already fastened under her seat-belt. "Right? Off?" she said, "I've done the burglar-alarm and dropped back the keys. Quick. Off."

James looked over his shoulder once quickly, blinked at the old white lilac tree, swung in, started the engine. They sped fast down the hill, through the edges of the town, through the next fat silent suburb, each house surrounded by its square of garden, all the people sleeping. They flew on past Sutton, past Cheam, past Kingswood, to the top of Reigate Hill and down to the motorway that slashes the last beautiful valley in Surrey; no sound except now and then a querulous mew from the back seat and the occasional creak of basket and re-arrangement of furry anatomy. This too stopped.

"He's a good cat," said James, "No fuss."

"Let's hope he settles. *Had* she a dog?"

"No. No, there wasn't a dog. I couldn't see one anyway. I think she was a bit uncertain whether she had one or not. I think she just remembers now and then that there's something you do before bedtime that ends off the day. Something to do with walking round the streets and pausing and thinking at lamp-posts. I'd guess the dog died years ago."

"What did she say?"

"Just meandered on. Said she'd heard we were moving. She seemed to know where. She asked when."

"She didn't know? That it was now? Actually now? Did you tell her?"

"No, I just said that we were soon pushing off. Setting sail to Kent, and she said, 'Ah, a new start. You must be wondering now if it's wise.' "

"What did she mean? We're not so very old. James will you stop?"

"Stop?"

"Fiddling with the radio. You know it's broken."

"It works sometimes. I'll get it fixed. I meant to but there's been no – ." There was a sudden, hideous crackling that turned to a piercing and persistent scream.

"*James*! Turn it off!"

"Sorry."

"If we want something to take our minds – . I'll put in a tape."

"I just wondered if I could get the World Service news."

"News? Why news?"

"Oh, I don't know. Just something Mrs Apse said. But she's crazy."

"How odd. I don't somehow see Mrs Apse being interested in the news. I suppose it's pretty good at over eighty to be bothering –."

"It was a news-flash she'd heard. They'd broken in to the late programmes with it. Just before midnight."

"What was it? The end of the world? It's rather like the end of the world, isn't it? There's nothing on the road – not even lights. Aren't the stars huge. Oh!"

Lights came flashing and twirling from behind them, up the road and a police-car came alongside. Slowed. Police faces looked at them, two discs above white shirt-sleeves. "It's stopping," said James, "What have we done?"

But the police-car changed its mind, picked up speed and was in a moment curving away to the left towards the Medway. Soon they saw the reason, for at the junction just before the river there was a house on fire, a clamour of engines and cars; silhouettes of men running. Flames sprang up from what in the darkness looked like a gabled mansion not unlike the one they'd left, but standing in fields.

"Oh, heavens," said Elisabeth. Her head full of the transience of houses, tears began again. "James," she said blinking, sitting straight, thinking of Dame Peggy Ashcroft, "What was it Mrs Apse said? About the news-flash?"

"Oh, just nonsense. There's been some sort of leak from a power station."

"What – an atomic leak?"

"Yes."

"A big one?"

"Yes. So she said. Chernobil affair."

"How awful. In Russia?"

"No. No – not according to Mrs Apse."

"Where?"

"Here."

"Here? What – England?"

"Yes."

"*Where*?"

"Hythe," he said, "Dungeness. But I can't believe it. She's more than likely to have got it wrong. Probably dreamt it. She said, 'The Kent coast, Dungeness.' It's probably the Orkneys or Loch Ness. Probably not England at all. East Germany. The Duchy of Hesse."

"There isn't a Duchy of Hesse. James – if it's Hythe – ."

He said nothing but began to twiddle the knob of the radio again. This time the crackling was less manic, but very steady.

"James – Hythe is where we are going."

"No it's not. Hythe's fifty miles from where we're going."

"But fifty miles is nothing. At Chernobil – ."

"They evacuated only thirty miles around Chernobil."

"So, we're moving to within twenty miles of the death-zone."

"Mrs Apse," said James, "Mrs Lapse, Mrs Per – Apse, is a dotty old woman who isn't even sure whether she has a dog or not. If there had been a major nuclear leak we would know it by now."

"How?"

"Well – there'd be – . We'd see it in the sky."

"Would we? From here? It's not a bomb. A leak isn't a mushroom cloud. Even a cloud we wouldn't see in the dark."

"We should have heard it."

"Should we? I don't think it is always an explosion. Even a big leak. Look at Sellafield. I don't think people a hundred miles from Chernobil saw anything. That's what was so eerie. A blast, a blaze, at first just white-hot concrete. The air clear. The birds singing. They didn't even announce Chernobil – ."

"They didn't announce it because spontaneous announcement is not a Russian habit."

"But it is, with us. We did. We have. We have announced Hythe. It is that huge reactor off-shore at Dungeness you look at while you're bathing. And it's in the same part of Kent where we are going to live."

"Mrs Apse," said James, turning off to Detling at the sign that says "You are now in Eastern Kent," "Mrs Coll – Apse is a mad old woman."

"That's what I think she isn't," said Elisabeth. "She heard the news-flash, connected the place with us and wandered round in case we were there. It's what she meant when she said that we were probably not feeling like leaving. James – we should go back. Towards London. Or to the North. James look – any traffic there's been, except the police-car, it's all been going the other way. To the North."

"We can't go back. The house is not ours any more. We dropped the keys back through the letter-box. And where on earth would we go if we turned North? And all the furniture coming trundling down to Kent tomorrow morning?"

"We could wake someone up. At home. In the road. They're probably expecting us back."

"They are all asleep. They'd think we were insane. They'd say, 'Ah, the menopausal move. A moving-of-house in late middle-age can turn the brain and it has at last turned Elisabeth's'."

157

"I don't care. We should turn back. James. We're driving right into the heart of it. Soon there'll be road-blocks."

"We are very tired," he said. "We don't have any judgment. You are manufacturing a nightmare. Your beloved erstwhile analyst would probably say that you are doing it to rest the mind from what we have done."

"Done?"

"Moved off from our life."

"Yes. Yes. That is what we have done, isn't it? We have elected to die."

He said, "We moved because the house had become huge and lonely. The children had gone. The town had changed so that you couldn't buy a packet of envelopes because all the little shops had become estate-agents. Two close friends had gone away ahead of us and we saw ourselves about to turn into a lovely old couple who had been in that house since before the Punic Wars. Toddling into old age. We wanted a fresh start. We wanted fresh-air. We wanted to set sail."

"We were trying to avoid reality," she said.

He said, "You are being morbid, neurotic and a bore."

Later on he said more kindly, "When we get there I will telephone somebody. Anyone you like. The Ministry of Defence. One of the children. Old Arthur at the Cabinet Office. I promise you."

She said, "You won't be able to telephone. They're not going to connect the phone until tomorrow."

Up Detling Hill there is even in the clearest weather nearly always mist, sometimes thick fog. Tonight, as they turned from the motorway landscape into the hills and fields of Kent the mist rolled towards them and surrounded them, the headlights slamming back in their faces a dazzle from a solid white blanket. Down the other side of the dual carriage-way, hidden partly by the trees of the central reservation as well as by the mist, there seemed all at once to be trundling a multitude of lorries. A high convoy.

"Whatever's that?"

"Just stuff coming up from the docks. Dover."

"At this time of night? D'you think – , d'you think it's lorries turning back?"

"I shall say again," said James, "And I shall continue to say it: Mrs Apse is a mad old woman, much taken up with death, as she should be at her age because it can't be far off; and she has been concerning herself with the end of the world. The local example at the moment of passing from one stage to another, of setting sail, of dying – for she's used to that: almost all her friends have done it – is us. After thirty years, we are voluntarily moving away from the town, the sweet South-London suburb, they all have come to believe is the only place anyone could want to live. We are thought to be rehearsing our death, leaving all we love. This has much occupied the mind of Mrs Apse and so she has come a-wandering through the leafy streets at night to stand at our garden gate and warn us like Cassandra that there is no advantage in trying to escape our ends. The bogeyman will get us. She is a busy-body. She is a busy bogey-body. I want nothing to do with her."

"And she imagined the news-flash?"

"Without the least doubt she imagined the news-flash."

The A20. The A2. The old pilgrims' road. The beginnings of the old Dutch architecture, and the Eastward sweep towards Canterbury where the fields begin to look like France: the most international piece of England where foreigners are not foreign for they have been landing and looking-round, fight-ing and passing through, trading and settling for thousands of years. James and Elisabeth side-stepped Canterbury but looked North once or twice to try to catch sight of the cathedral, the mighty ship in the meadows behind the Sturry gasometer.

"We must have missed it," Elisabeth said.

"It won't be lit up at night," said James.

"Isn't it? How d'you know?"

159

"The expense. Of course not. Nobody in Canterbury would be able to sleep for the light."

"It's lit up for occasions. Special occasions."

"Then, take heart."

"You mean – if there's been a – Chernobil, it would be lit up?"

"Any Science-Fiction you care to read," said James, "To do with the end of the world, has a reference to packed churches. If the town of Hythe had gone up this evening in white heat, Canterbury would have been – made available."

"Not if the electricity – James, the road. It is so dark – ."

"Of course the road is dark, it is two o'clock in the morning. Anyway, look. There's light coming up ahead."

And at Bekesbourne Lane roundabout, light was blazing, though disconcertingly, for as they drove towards it there was another house on fire. People in a clump stood in the road, humped in blankets like refugees. Black rafters threw scarves of flame carelessly into the sky. Firemen waved the car furiously by over the boa-constrictors of the hoses.

"A second fire," said Elisabeth.

"Atomic leaks don't cause outbreaks of spontaneous combustion," said James.

She said, "How do you know?"

They turned off and drove between young orchards, miles of flat-topped apple-trees whitening into flower, acres of precise geometry behind the intertwined windbreaks of the poplars. They flew on through the beautiful, industrious landscape. Elisabeth said, 'Doesn't it? How do we know? What do we know about anything?"

" 'Only a man harrowing clods'," said James.

"What?"

"I'm talking about eternity. Poem. 'At the Time of the Breaking of Nations'. This is a wonderful place we're coming to live in. We both know it is. Hopeful. Busy. All the pruning. Always getting ready for the next season. Kent's a *wonderful* place. Oh, stop thinking of doom."

"If it was only nations breaking," she said, "And clods aren't harrowed any more. I don't know when I've seen a clod being harrowed."

He held her hand, " 'Only a maid and her wight'," he said, " 'Go whispering by. Wars annals will cloud into night ere their story die'."

"Yes," she said, "Love goes on. But this is worse than war."

"You are tired," said James and turned left, then right and they flew through the villages: Littlebourne and Bramling, Wingham, Rusham and Shatterling and Ash. Hop-poles stood black and abstract and the rising moon shone on them. The chocolatey ridges of a great field lay wide open for corn.

Up a brow and down a brow they flew. Long stands of high, whippy trees sharp across a horizon. Up and down and across the last miles of silt that had once been lapping sea. To the north the great pots of Richborough cooling-towers loomed over the flint lumps of Roman fort. To the south, meadows where cows stood thinking in the dark. In this moonlight and shadow Elisabeth's darkness at last lifted away. "Nearly there," said James.

"Left here, oh, left *here*," she said, and down a narrow street, between mediaeval houses, roofs in an ancient clutter, the masts of fishing boats angular at a street corner they came quietly, slowly in to the old town.

"I'll take the cat," she said, "Let him run round the garden a bit. Then he can sleep with us tonight." James unlocked the door in the rose-garden wall. They watched the shadow of the cat, then gathered it up and James unlocked the side door of their new home.

"No lights! James! No *lights*!" but "Look," said ever-ready James with a torch, shining it upwards. "He was the meanest man that ever sold a house but I thought that people who took the light-bulbs were a myth."

He held Elisabeth's hand and they made their way through the rooms that lay waiting for tomorrow. The sitting-room smelt of cherry-wood. Up the stairs they went, along the ancient landing to the one room they had made ready, crossing its drunken floor.

Elisabeth wandered about, came back to the room, let drop Dame Peggy Ashcroft's woollen suit and walked over it as she went to lie down on the bed. "You should take off your clothes properly," said James. She said, "James – such incredible joy. All the years. Ridiculous to be afraid. It has all been so – ," and was asleep.

He took off her shoes and then his own and watched the sky through the little windows, listening for the sound of the church-bells that the town was famous for. Waiting for the chime he swam in to the dark.

Above him there was a flurry and scuttering in the roof. Starlings in new nests under the eaves. The cat jumped softly on to the sill and looked upwards with optimism. "Must clear those birds out," said James in dreams and Elisabeth in dreams said "Birds – ."

She woke to his empty bed, the dazzle of morning. Silence. Silence. In the garden flowers throbbed and shone. She opened the window on to them and the next world.